Willi

C000173890

www.williamknight.info

X Y Z

First published in 2019
William Knight

Second One Hundred

Copyright © 2019 William Knight
www.williamknight.info

978-0-473-48574-0 (Softcover)
978-0-473-48575-7 (ePub)
978-0-473-48576-4 (Kindle)
978-0-473-48577-1 (PDF)
978-0-473-48578-8 (iBook)

This book is licensed for your personal enjoyment only. No part of this publication may be reproduced, re-sold or given away to other people. If you would like to share this book, please purchase an additional copy for each recipient. If you're reading this book and did not purchase it, or it was not purchased only for your own use, then please purchase your own copy. Thank you for respecting the hard work of this author.

This book is a work of fiction. Names, characters, businesses, organisations, places and events are either the product of the authors imagination or are used fictitiously. Any resemblance to actual persons, living or dead, events or locations is entirely coincidental.

For two exceptional zoomers in my life
Morgan and Fern

The Generations

Generation X – "GenX" Born 1964–1980

Generation Y – "Millennials" Born 1981–1996

Generation Z – "Zoomers" Born 1996–present day

Prologue

Humans have inflicted terrible miseries on each other over the centuries. From the Second World War, to the slave trade, and to government-inflicted famines. But civilisation has never been so damaged as when some arse invented emojis.

At a stroke of evil genius, grown adults rushed to form sideways faces from punctuation and add cartoon rolling eyes to the middle of otherwise serious messages. We fear misunderstanding and must explain ourselves with miniature pictures. But if you have to point out your jokes, cannot express your emotions, are unable to construct arguments, or are otherwise challenged with words, then perhaps you should pick up the phone — and not the smart one either — the one with the coiled wire and a receiver.

The death of *real* conversation was funny at the beginning, I admit, but has since gone bonkers. Emojis have spilt out of emails and into work meetings. *Jazz hands*, a symbol of overexcitement, together with *yay*, have become prayers to company leadership. I've seen gangs of otherwise sensible computer programmers offering up ten wiggly fingers to the dull clichés of management. Awful.

And we've all become so tied up in responding to emojis they no longer mean anything. We all know that anything finishing with *LOL* — not an emoji, apparently, but who's counting — almost certainly did *not* get you laughing out loud. You might have offered an amused snort, or a smile on the inside of your mouth, but a full-on laugh out loud was as likely as Facebook paying all its tax.

Recently, I had the displeasure of seeing a dancing poo at the end of an email. What happened to fifty years of growing up, leaving the anal phase, and not looking down the toilet to make sure I did a good job. I've had wives, girlfriends, children, heartaches and I've lost people I loved. Am I expected to find amusement in a dancing poo? No!

Emojis are some of the many things I detest about modern life and modern tech. I detest the internet; my mobile phone; the infantilising of society by cat video; being online twenty-four hours a day; and that to progress your career you're advised (by online gurus) to spend your evenings posting observations to compete with a million other jostling halfwits all doing the same thing.

And everything is in the open — on blogs, or Facebook, or Twitter — a reaction, feedback, critical conversation, a profile, news, fake news, lies, laughs, memes, themes, threads and vines. So much is available that nobody has time to digest anything. When everything is *out there*, nothing is *out there*.

To get with the pathetic attention spans of modern life, even the *Guardian* has had to make its pieces shorter and reach the point sooner. Sometimes they are so short it's as if they didn't bother to write the copy but simply posted the journalist's first paragraph of notes.

The publication carries a weekly article called *The long read*. After all, it's better not to surprise readers with a piece of writing they don't have the concentration for. No. Best not. Prepare them. Let the reader know in advance they will have to commit several minutes to get through all the words.

I imagine the water cooler discussions the next day, among the millennials:

"Yeah, Cuz, I got through *The long read* yesterday."

[Jazz hands.] "Yay, Bro. The whole thing?"

[Nods.] "Whole thing — you know — the important bits."

"Cool. You crazy mofo."

"Yeah." [Fills cup from cooler.]

"You time for an Americano later?"

"I'm hanging more gifs on my profile. Message me?"

"Sick. Laters."

The world's gone insane and I'm right in the middle of it. Too young to retire, too old to work in these fucked-up, alt-corporate millennial environments, but desperate for the money to pay for two homes, a probable divorce and grown-up kids who blame me and my generation for wrecking their lives — and the planet while we were at it.

I'm not sure when I became part of the older generation, but here I am. Somehow Gen Y became the cool Millennials and Gen X became old, technically-challenged farts? One minute I am the technical wizard, the next I can't get my phone to work and am bamboozled by giphys and emoticons and emojis. I don't know what they mean, when to use what, and a wrong key press gets my so-called *thread* bombarded with capital letters and, of course, rolling eyes.

But I'm one of the original computer geeks. One of the guys who got past the tenth screen on *Space Invaders* and had my initials, JAK, as the high score on every Asteroids machine from Boscombe Pier to the Bear Hotel on Maidenhead High Street. I solved the *Monkey Coconut Problem* on a ZX81 — no mean feat in just 1K of memory.

I was in the first intake for Computer Science O Level at my local college, and I signed up for a computer programming degree when the rest of the world was still using slide rules and copying documents in purple ink.

When my mum threw a party to celebrate my leaving home to go to university, my aunt came up to me, holding a prawn cocktail in a wine glass, and said, "Computers, that's the new thing isn't it?"

She got it. I was part of a small wave of silicon-brained cool kids that was destined to become a tsunami. My generation was going to make the world a better place and in record time. We had ideas of perfect information, total transparency, evidence-based-government and university for all. We were the builders of Utopia and the founders of global prosperity. We were Gods.

"Yeah, I guess," I said.

I hadn't then realised the destiny for which I was headed. It was nothing more than fun. Fun to spend 10p on a video game and bash the console into submission. Fun to program pretty patterns on a screen and load games from a floppy disk, and fun to be part of the BBC's *Micro Live* phenomenon, when the broadcaster sponsored its own computer as part of its remit to educate the masses.

And it remained fun until it became a trap, when computers ceased to be the promise of progress and instead became the terrorists of truth. Somewhere along the way, I turned from God of Silicon to an anorak-wearing dweeb, and from dweeb to a lonely fifty-five-year-old bastard. One at the end of his career, hopelessly out of touch, and unable to operate his own phone.

WTF happened?

1

I get up early, ready for the first day in my new job. It's bright. Fuck it! The sun is rising over The Downs and mist is drifting across the long grass.

But this nature stuff hardly registers. My brain hurts from the bottle-and-a-half of red wine I downed last night, to accompany a chicken vindaloo, in front of the TV. What was I watching? Some Japanese woman folding pants into matchboxes, then *Newsnight*. I fell asleep, and since I live on my own and there's nobody to wake me up and ask me sweetly to join them between the sheets. I rolled into bed about two-thirty.

By the time I make it to the office and hang around in the double-height reception, I'm thinking a bit more clearly. And I'm thinking that I'm too old for this type of humiliation. I'm a new starter turning up early in a suit, sitting on one of the vibrant-green sofas scattered artfully around the area, waiting for an HR person.

I straighten my tie and tuck my shirt in behind my braces. I sigh. I inspect the impressively high-ceilinged atrium, the sleek white walls and the glass-fronted entrance. A mezzanine runs the length of one side and people are cutting across from one half of the building to the other. It's clean. Tidy. One wall has a huge purple neon sign saying, *Go For It*. Corporate slogan, I guess. Sigh.

With each successive job in my career, it has taken me less time to become cynical and annoyed. In the early days, I was excited to start at new places. Excited to meet my new colleagues and excited to uncover the hidden workings of the firm. I wanted to get to my desk and begin digging around in their source code. I wanted to please the customers and delight the company owners. I was fresh faced and keen. Nauseating, even.

At my very first software firm we coded microprocessors for the automotive industry and wrote applications to control their supply lines. Everything was new and original. Nothing we did had been done before. It was creative innovation at the cutting edge. We could barely explain it to ourselves, let alone to our mates or girlfriends. It was called a computer language, but that suggests other people could understand it. They couldn't. Everything we did was obscure, opaque, designed as we went along and thrown into production the minute it worked once. It was art. One-offs. Commissions. The stuff we wrote was interpretation. It wasn't a language or a code; it was a feeling. And it was great.

But today I'm cynical about the new job before I've even started. It'll be the same old bollocks dressed up in a different corporate colour; a slight variation to the usual set of aspirational values that nobody remembers past one read of the memo. Something about pushing the limits, learning for life and caring for your colleagues. *Go For It.* Fucking marvellous.

"Jack. Hi. Lovely to see you again. Welcome to Sweet. You look smart."

Amber's smile shines like the earlier sun through the window. I want to pull the curtains some more. I stop myself forming a crucifix with my fingers to ward her off.

She offers a hand.

I've changed my mind. I've had second thoughts and won't be taking the job after all. I've had a better offer. I'm going to pick my arse for a bit in preference. Or maybe I'll spend time staring at creases in the bathroom lino. Or perhaps I'll take some catatonia-inducing drugs and lie on the floor.

But I say, "Hi, Amber. It's great to be here. Did I overdo it with the suit?" I take her hand and we shake, briefly and professionally. Thank God she didn't fist bump or slip me some skin.

I have on a dark-brown, Rupert-check, two-piece with black shoes and braces. The suit is a gentle nod to Rupert-the-bear; not the kind of exaggerated yellow check that he wore, but a broad thread in a subtly lighter colour. Probably, nobody else can see it. It's my interview and first-day suit. I kid myself it's okay, but I know it's ten years old and suspect it looks terrible.

"You'll get the hang of it. We're pretty informal here. Non-corporate is a motto," says Amber. Grin.

I've fucked up, is what she means. But I can see from the over-designed, matching colour scheme that they're so non corporate they've gone full circle and become the very epitome of corporate. They'd slavishly followed a trend started in West Coast USA, thirty years ago, thinking they were irreverent nonconformists, and have become a boring, same-old-same-old corporation trying too hard to deny its true identity.

In any case, what she doesn't know is that I chose the suit to stand out. To be different. To detach myself from the retro-T-shirt-and-hoodie intake of millennial IT professionals. I have dressed elegantly to remember a more civilised age — albeit one from only ten years ago.

It fleetingly crosses my mind that my clothing rebellion is sufficiently nonconformist that I ought to fit in perfectly at this alt-corporate homage to modernity. I try to ignore the thought. That way lies insanity. It's the line of thinking that says anarchy is logically impossible because the idea of *no laws* is a law. That means it can't possibly be anarchy. Everything falls into the anarchy trap.

Amber looks like she's following my mind vortex. I imagine she's saying, *There's nothing too wacky in this place. To exclude yourself by being too wacky is, in fact, to fit in perfectly. You cannot be so out there that you aren't accepted in here.*

Unless you are old.

"I like to wear a suit from time to time," I say. "It's one of the few luxuries men are still allowed."

She looks at me through a sideways smile and slightly narrowed dog-like eyes. I wonder if she has Rottweiler ancestry. I'm sure she's thinking, *You're an old git. How did you get the job?*

I smile back. I worry that my greying sideburns and sartorial choices appear less modern than they do ancient bastard.

I met Amber a month ago, at the interview. I had to hide my cynicism deep inside and pretend to be interested in the job. It was easy. I *was* interested. Six months out of work, two dependent adult children — well one of them is dependent — an estranged wife and double housing to pay for, and living on the streets with a cardboard sign around your neck starts to become a realistic outcome.

Or you can get a job.

I'd tried to get a job before this one, of course. But I was beginning to think I was too old and, frankly, too old-fashioned.

The particularly trying recruitment agent, who had a pair of rodent-like teeth the size of the Twin Towers, asked if I'd link in. I was flattered, I suppose. Despite the teeth, and her tedious nature, she wasn't bad looking, and me and

Caroline had been separated for months.

"Well, yes, why not?" I smiled. "Coffee or wine?"

I got a look like I'd experimented on baby orangutans.

"No. LinkedIn. Your LinkedIn account?"

I had minimal recall. "Not a drink? Do you mean link-up?"

"No. LinkedIn."

There was a shameful silence.

Then she said, "But you have a great LinkedIn profile."

I chewed through a few of my memories. Facebook. The kids used Instagram. Twitter. My banking website. I had an Oyster card, once.

"No," I said. It was an admission of failure, but also, looking back, one of curiosity. Linking in, like a chain. And then a faint recollection stirred. Something about marketing and sales. I remembered one of the salespeople at Fergusons (my old engineering job) talking about how he'd used it to get business in Germany.

"No," I said, "I'm not a salesperson. Never really liked the idea." I smiled.

She laughed. A small laugh through her nostrils, before her better judgement kicked in and she brought her rat-face under control. "You're so modest. You know everybody has to have a LinkedIn account. Everybody is a sales person. Everybody has something to sell. You, Jack, are selling your skills as a computer professional. And you did a really good job." Full on smile, as if she thought I was joking.

Her certainty made me sort through my memories again, and I recalled my daughter setting something up for me.

"Oh. LinkedIn. Yes. Yes. Of course."

How could I forget, it's what got me the new job. Fake youth supplied by my daughter. It was the first thing Amber

9

mentioned when we met for the interview. She "absolutely loved" my LinkedIn profile. It hadn't clicked.

"You've taken so much care to set out your experience, and we just loved the bit about your family," she said.

"Thanks."

I didn't admit I hadn't actually seen it. I wondered what Em had written.

Amber takes me up to the first floor, where my new team are expecting me. I follow dutifully, and because I'm nervous I overdo saying hello. I say "Hello" in the lift and as we pass people in random passages. I don't know why I'm putting myself through this. It's hell. I get a few responses, but mostly people just smile and nod, and look at me strangely.

"How many people work here now?" I ask. I know the business has been expanding recently. It split from an online auction website when they began selling banking services, and has been through a year-long growth spurt. This much came out of the interview with the agent and the small bit of research I conducted.

"New people start every week. Almost every day. It's amazing. We've taken the ground and first floor and are trying to get the third. It's such a great place to work."

I nod. I probably mouth *Wow*, but no sound comes out. I don't see that fast expansion makes for a *great* place to work. I think her logic is mucked up. It's a symptom of the excessive optimism this place exudes.

"This is your area," she says, as we walk into an open-plan office space.

Desks align in pods of six or so, interleaved with half a dozen vibrant-green sofas the same as the ones in reception. Vibrant green and purple are the corporate colours. I've seen them on posters all over the walls, and on the webpage. It's probably on the toilet walls.

People at the desks carry on working. We walk to a sofa between two rolling white boards covered in multi-coloured sticky squares — the type that have become ubiquitous in every IT office in the world.

"Vasi, this is Jack," says Amber.

Vasi, sitting on the sofa with a computer on his lap, has hair down to his elbows, a beard to rival Captain Birdseye's and is wearing a dog collar complete with spikes. He could be twenty-three or four.

"Hi, Jack," he says. "My pronouns of choice are they, them."

Interesting way to introduce yourself.

"Sure," I say. "I think my favourites are it and she."

I'm smiling. I enjoy the joke. I might have found somebody I can get on with by 9:30 on the first day. Result.

He looks at me like I have Black Death.

Amber pipes up. "No, Jack. Vasi means they like to be referred to as they or them. Gender neutral."

But he has a beard like Captain bloody Fishfinger's. I think I am open mouthed.

"You'll get used to it," says Vasi.

He — I mean they — hold out their hand. I don't know if I should shake, bump, or slip. Perhaps he's — fuck it, they're — expecting a double-cheek French thing with a hug. I take their hand and shake. It seems to be acceptable, because they smile and look up at Amber.

"Vasi's on your team. A great developer," she says.

"Good." I nod.

Introduction number one gone badly.

It's 9:35 a.m.

The rest of the morning proceeds as these things do, with moments of intense scrutiny as you are introduced to new people, followed by boredom with all the housekeeping. By lunchtime I'm sitting at my new desk surrounded by my team. I have Vasi, Jinny, Berry, Davy and Carl.

They are all in their twenties, except Carl, and don't look up much when introduced. Just a brief 'wassup' kind of greeting. They switch between mobile phones, tablets, laptops and face-to-face discussion in one smooth merry-go-round. It's like watching and listening to eight radio stations, four TVs, a record player and an intercom announcement all at once. It leaves me dizzy.

"Carl, can you show me how to switch this laptop on?" I laugh. "I can't work it out." I half expect him to point and snigger. To shout round the office about the ineptitude of his new boss who can't switch on the PC.

But he doesn't.

He reaches over and pushes a black button surrounded by black trim that lights up black. I'm reminded of Zaphod Beeblebrox when he boards Hot Black's stunt ship before plunging into the sun.

"It's a feature of these new Macs," Carl says. "A cool design."

Did he roll his eyes? I think he did.

I can relate to Carl. It's a normal name. He's normal to go with his name. He doesn't give me a pronoun selection, is dressed in a shirt with a collar and I know he has kids at home just from the rings under his eyes. Yes, he's younger than me, but he has Gen X written on his forehead. Gen X, born maybe fifteen or so years after me. His desk has a picture of his wife.

I take a breath.

Then he says, "I've got pole dancing at twelve. I don't suppose you want to join? It's great for core strength."

I'm about to burst into laughter, then I see it's not a joke.

I grimace, but disguise it as a smile as the corners of my mouth turn up. I imagine Carl in a g-string flicking his nipples with his tongue. My fingers are tingling. I can feel the blood rushing to my cheeks and the back of my neck burning. What den of misfits have I gone and landed in?

"It's great," he says. Jazz hands.

I feel like I'm in the dancing poo.

While the team are off for lunch, or pole dancing, or pulling tricks for all I know, I manage to get the computer started and begin reading the slew of emails that have arrived prior to my arrival. First day check-list. Induction appointment. Message from the owner. Wireless passwords. Wiki logon. Hello from Freya. Welcome to the Cast Champion's community of practice. All cast meetings. Friday night is screening night — though Friday is spelled *FriYAY* — practically makes me puke. And what the fuck is this *cast* thing?

I accept a few meetings that look like they might be for me, and notice that all the appointments are in rooms named after famous movies. I read the invitation titled *Induction Catchup* for a meeting that's due tomorrow in *Casablanca*. I get it *cast* as in staff. That's cute. Blahh.

"It's thrilling to have you join us Jack, and I hope you are settling in [*smiley face, jazz hands*]. I'm Freya, your designated Cast Champion or CC, but Amber's standing in for me while I'm on my pet therapy day. I've put a catchup in your calendar for tomorrow. I'll see you then. Yay. [*Jazz hands*]"

I look forward to that.

My home life is based in a single-bed flat in the centre of town. The entrance is nestled between Oxfam and a gents' hairdresser owned by one of my neighbours. The doorway can be messy on a Sunday, when people leave furniture on the street for the charity shop, but it's a solid, turn-of-the-last-century, red-brick building that was done up before I moved in. It's warm. I have a view of The Downs out of the back. And I have everything I need. A kitchen, bathroom, double bedroom, and a sofa in front of a small TV. I even salvaged my TV remote pouch from my wife. It hangs on the side of the sofa, so I don't lose the bloody things.

I think about what my parents paid for the family house when I was a boy, and compare it to what I have now. It's not a comparison I like to dwell on for long. When my parents divorced, we had two family homes of equal size and that wasn't unusual — or it didn't seem to be.

I'm not poor, compared to many.

I do okay.

But I'm worse off than my parents. Sure, we can now buy unheard-of magical items my parents couldn't have dreamed of, but the money goes on talking speakers and doorbell cameras you can watch from work, and endless subscriptions to things you forget about but which were intended to make life easier, draining the weekly budget with slow drips like Chinese water torture. I'm told that for two pounds a month you can subscribe to an app to tell you when the bus is coming and use your phone to track the journey. What happened to timetables and windows?

It's been a while since I've been on a bus, though, and that's because I've been unemployed for a bit and everything I need is within walking distance. I can even walk to the new job, which is a bonus. If I ever do need a car, it's parked at the wife's place — my ex-place.

But what's best about my flat is the pub, and that's another reason to go everywhere on foot. It's one hundred yards down the road. *The Flying Pig.*

I know, right. What a fucking stupid name for a pub. It used to be called *The King's Head.* A solid traditional name you can't muck about with. The sort of name that shrieks warm beer and the distant clunk of leather on willow. It probably had a medieval poet in residence, and King Charles stayed there before being divested of his head by an axe. It's the sort of pub name that gives you confidence in being British and takes away any lingering doubts about colonialism or slave-trade sponsorship, or Brexit. In short, it's the sort of pub name that makes you want to pop in for a pint and end up staying behind locked doors until 2 a.m.

Pubs went through a transformation in the wake of the smoking ban, and many closed down as a result. Those that were left evolved into gastro-pubs or cafe-cum-bar type things. They needed to appeal to those millennials I'm so fond of, so the thousand-year-old British pub names were replaced with ironic, shallow marketing gimmicks. I imagine the next evolution of pub names will be shallower still. *The Jazz Hands. The Rolling Eyes. The Dancing Poo.* Deep sigh.

Luckily, beneath the ironic, post-truth exterior of *The Flying Pig* is hidden a traditional pub with oak beams, plastered walls and brass, heavy-horse medallions. I ignore the fact this interior has probably been carefully *designed* with the old-bastard clientele of the area in mind. I've not inspected the brass nick-nacks for authenticity and I never will. This is one fake bubble I don't intend to burst.

As usual, the publican, Larry, is behind the bar drying pint glasses with a tea-towel. His grey ponytail and goatee beard over deep wrinkles make him look like the ghost of a lost biker that died from smoking, but he's a comforting presence in this establishment. I'd trust him with any drunken talk that came out of my gob, and he looks as if he's useful if there's ever any trouble. Which I've never seen here; perhaps because of how Larry is built.

"Jack. Usual?"

I nod.

Larry bought the pub as a retirement business a few years back and runs it as if the nineteen fifties are still in full swing. He's told me he'd like to bring back a men's smoking room but *those fucking politicians* won't allow it. I swear he has a tea towel growing out of his fingers, because he's always drying pint glasses when I walk in. Perhaps he has an app that shows when customers are on their way and thinks the tea-towel drying routine adds authenticity and will expand his profit margin. Who knows? I haven't asked.

I like to think Larry is a friend, but it might be the £4.40, I've been paying per pint several times an evening lately. I read that the British public think the average pint is 60p too much. It's universal. If you pay three quid for your beer you think it should be £2.40 and if you live in London and pay £5.50 for a pint — God forbid — you think you should only pay £4.90. This shows how well those marketers are doing. They have successfully tailored their product to gain the maximum the market will bear. Forget old fogey concepts of costs plus a little profit. They will squeeze out whatever they can. It's surprising that supermarkets aren't asking you for a statement of earnings then setting prices based on what you can afford to pay. They will. What do you think those loyalty cards are all about? Why do you think they are so interested in you filling a trolley and scanning the goods yourself? It's so they can make prices up as you approach the till, and they're working on the tech to make it possible.

Larry draws me a pint of IPA and puts it down on the green beer towel laid along the bar.

"How's the new job?" he asks.

I pick up the pint and take a sip. The job's shit full of crazies. It's a place where the most normal are the abnormal ones. It's a place where *jazz hands* are currency and shiny shoes are dirt. It's a place where work comes second to social media and you're never sure why you are getting paid or how they make money. It's a place where you can spend your time doing whatever you want as long as you present your non achieving with a morning *yay*. It's a place I won't fit in for a million years, only then if I'm dead and my bones are re-purposed as part of the pool table.

"Early days," I say. "Seems okay." I take a gulp. I don't share everything with Larry. Not until I'm on my third pint.

The IPA slides down my throat and hits my brain cells almost immediately. It's like going home to a soft bed and a loving partner.

I take another gulp.

And another.

Truth is, I'm bored. In fact, I am more than bored. I am unable to react to things. I don't care. Don't see the point in doing anything. Over the last few years, I've stopped all my hobbies, I've lost all my friends and my family. When the doctor put me on citalopram, I lost the last bit of self-control I had for exercise or overeating. I started putting on weight. My career was going nowhere and I was constantly arguing with management over things I didn't give a fuck about. And when, on those odd occasions I did give a fuck about something, I didn't know whether to blame myself for not caring all the time, or for caring so much that I caused an argument.

First day at the new job. And I don't care.

"Get the next couple lined up, Larry," I say. "Loads to talk about."

2

I'm woken by the doorbell.

It's 10 a.m.

I realise I didn't put the alarm on, and then remember I came home pissed and decided I wasn't going to bother.

The doorbell chimes once more. It's an irritating chime that reminds me of the fake marimba sound on a 1980s synthesiser. I think I know who's there.

"Come on up, Emmy," I say into the door-opening phone-like thing at the entrance — I've never known what those things are called: an intercom? I don't know.

I open the door and leave it ajar then go into the kitchen to put the kettle on. My head thumps like it's been in a real game of Karate Champ.

Em arrives. She's not looking happy.

She hugs me. "Hi, Dad." But there's no warmth. It's just going through the family meeting process. "Why aren't you at work?"

Oh that. Yes, well. I was talking to Larry at *The Flying Pig* and decided the job was a total waste of my time. They are a bunch of social misfits with no idea about how the real world works or why it works. I can't stand the culture, the film-making metaphor makes me sick and I've no fucking idea what's going on.

"I didn't feel so well, this morning," I say. "I thought I'd better take the day off. Wouldn't want to spread it around the office in my first week." I laugh. "Not a good impression."

"You mean you were down the pub, got drunk and decided you'd rather waste your time sitting on your backside doing nothing and getting pickled in a jar of beer!"

My daughter has insight beyond her years.

I pour water into the coffee cups, stir, hand her one and she follows me into the lounge.

I sit down.

She stays standing. Looking over me. Judging.

I take a sip of coffee and look up at her. She's wearing a short Royal Stewart tartan skirt over white tights with cherry-red, eight-hole Dr Martens. I know they have eight holes because I've counted them. When I was a kid the measure of how hard you were was the number of holes in your DMs. She's hard.

She cements this hard exterior with a run of earrings on her left ear and a single, pointed stud in her right. Her dyed-red hair is shaved on one side and long on the other. Asymmetric, apparently. The ensemble is completed with a white T-shirt emblazoned with *Extinction Rebellion* under a black second-hand leather jacket. She's a throwback to the great British punk traditions of the seventies, but with a post-truth twist that I don't understand.

I love her dearly.

"Come on, Dad. This is shit. Don't bounce this one."

I don't know what I can say. Actually, I'm not sure what she said. I stare at the coving. I stroke my unshaved chin.

"You have to get your act together. Fake it 'til you make it. Come on. Mum says you used to love going to work …"

She pauses for a long while. I'm concerned about what's coming next.

"… but that it all changed when you had me and Geronimo."

I don't say anything.

"Did you want me and my brother?"

I stare at her. Fucking hell! What a thing to ask. Jesus! I sip coffee to cover the discomfort and she stares back at me with *disappointed* written in her face.

Until recently the kids thought I was a hopeless dinosaur, because I fought constantly to get them off their devices and engage with the real world. They laughed at the idea of playing chess or Scrabble or talking about politics. Every evening, I spent alone. The kids in their own world, my wife in hers, and me watching telly. My family had been split apart by the internet and yet we still lived in the same house. If we could have virtualised our living space and put it in the cloud, three-quarters of my family would have done it without thinking, and I would have been left by myself holding the Scrabble box with sellotaped corners and a missing J.

"Of course, Em," I say.

"Really, Dad? You don't always act like it."

I couldn't help comparing their childhood to my own. I was the youngest of three boys, and I don't remember playing inside except when it was raining so hard we couldn't physically get into the garden because of the flooding on the lawn. And the flooding and rain only added to the games. We made carts, and we put polythene roofs on them with plastic nicked from a building site — there was always a building site somewhere, with scaffolding planks and tin sheets and all manner of stuff we made camps from or cut up for tree houses.

Okay, *sometimes* we were inside. We watched the BBC's *Multi-Coloured Swap Shop* on alternate Saturday mornings, and ITV's *Tiswas* on the others — we couldn't agree which, so Mum made us alternate. But often the programmes would inspire us to get outside and play in the garden. Most of our games were invented on the spot or we added rules to standard games to make them funnier, or fairer, or more interesting. The rules came from the playing and the playing created the rules.

We built catapults to shoot each other, camps to hide in, bats to play cricket with; we used cans for football and for *kick-the-can* — I think other kids used to call it *prisoner*, or something — but *kick-the-can* did exactly what it said on the tin. We made marble runs from builder's sand, Hungarian goulash from mud, bows and arrows from bamboo, snail houses from grass and sticks, targets from bricks and slides from plastic. And when all that failed, we had our push bikes for motocross.

I didn't know any different, but my childhood weekends were paradise. What more could a boy have asked from life than to have two ready-made mates who wanted to do the same thing at the same time, and if they didn't, we threw stones at a bottle to see who got to decide?

What father would not want this for his kids?

But my kids rejected it, and the parents around me rejected it. It was lame. I was lame. I was out of touch with modern children. But as I saw the kids tied to increasingly expensive devices, I died a little every day. I was ashamed I wasn't in control of their growing up and mortified at how little they seemed to actually play.

In their eyes, I was controlling and pointless and disappointing.

It's not supposed to be this way. I know that. Kids aren't supposed to be disappointed in their fathers. It's *supposed* to be the other way round. The parents are disappointed in the child. And then one day the kid comes home with a new vigour, after university or a round-the-world trip, or after the experimental careers have all failed, or the drugs have been banished — whatever it is, it's something which the parents disapproved of but the child was desperate to use as a stamp of autonomy. Anyway, at some point the child's choices are vindicated, the parents back off, everybody coos and the parent-child relationship is reborn as one of equals, even as friends. It's Hollywood, but it's what we all expect. It's what I expected, anyway.

And I suppose that did happen with Em. Just not with … well, more of that later.

"Of course, I wanted you. I even wanted your brother," I say, and then I realise how that sounds when I see her grimace.

"But not anymore?"

"No. No. Not that. It came out wrong. It's me, Em. I wanted more for you."

"But I have everything I need except a happy family. Because you moved out."

"You know I didn't move out from choice."

"Get woke, Dad!."

"What?"

"Look! Just get real. What the fuck. It was the drinking. And that was your choice. And now you're drinking to avoid the new job."

Yes, I had imagined her and her mother talking endlessly about the fucked-up, pointless, drunken husband and father. I bet they shared notes and stuck pins in a Ken doll.

But Em is right, I didn't move out so much as make it unbearable for everybody to live with me. Caroline threw me out. I deserved it. I got furious when the toothpaste ran out or the iPlayer started buffering. I got furious at anything and everything. I was just fucking furious. Caroline had no choice.

"Can you sit down, at least," I say. I've become very

aware of Em looking down on me like a black-capped judge. "Please. Let's talk." I point to the chair opposite.

The chair scrapes the lino as she pulls it back to sit down.

I confide in Em about the new job. I'm angry that these people can make a living where I've found it so hard to get work, even though I'm infinitely more experienced. I complain about the pace of change, the black on-off button, the company colours and logo. The whole thing suits me worse than a tutu in a snowstorm. I feel like I'm being forced into the cold, woefully underdressed and about to die.

"Dad. It's just a job. Yes, one that you need. But just a job. Seven-and-a-half hours a day. That's all. Do it, and come home. Even I have to be an adult sometimes." She laughs.

I laugh.

We talk more. We drink more coffee.

I'm expecting her to bring up the subject of her brother again, but am relieved when she doesn't. And I avoid mentioning him.

We just chat, and the hour we spend is a relief. Like something that was unsaid and frightening has lost its power, and now it's come out we can breathe again and get on with our lives. And that's how I feel. I feel better. Even the hangover is subsiding and I know I'll be able to get on with the day.

Em looks at her phone. "It's getting near to lunch, we need to get you into work," she says. "What do they wear?"

"Apart from the spiked dog-collars and tattoos, you mean?"

"They sound like my sort of people," she says.

She wanders into my bedroom and I hear her open the

wardrobe doors. "Dad, you've got to get some joy into your flat. This place is a tip and your wardrobe needs a sort out." I can hear her moving coat hangers about with that distinctive metal-sliding-on-metal sound, and she's talking about minimalist living through the joy of decluttering. It sounds utter shit.

She returns with a pair of jeans and a lime-green *Space Invaders* T-shirt. "You're gonna slay them in this. I bought it. Remember?"

I remember. I've worn it from time to time. I feel daft in it.

But since Em has chosen it, I get dressed and we walk out of the flat together.

I get to work and nobody mentions I've missed half the day. In fact, nobody is sitting at their desks. They are all *on stage* for the *all-cast* meeting going on in the atrium. I arrive just as the talking starts, and stand at the back as if I've been there all along.

A large TV is showing some slide show about market growth and customer satisfaction, or something. The head of product is talking.

"We've just hit a hundred thousand customers in the EU."

Yay! Jazz hands.

"Three months ahead of projections."

Yay! Jazz hands.

"The results of the customer survey are in, and we are number three, up two places in a month."

Yay! Jazz hands.

There's something infectious about the absolute, unquestioning enthusiasm. I find I'm smiling and clapping. Not just because Amber and the entire company are gathered, but because I feel a strange stirring in my stomach. It could be nausea, but I think it's genuine pleasure.

I put a stop to the feeling by looking around at the assembled employees. I have to be the oldest. I can see a dozen bearded and groomed millennial men — though who knows what pronoun they aspire to; a few younger punk rock types, a group in which my daughter would fit; thirty or so hoodie-wearing males in their twenties and early thirties; and an equal number of women in green T-shirts with slogans.

I am unremarkable in my own T-shirt. It's the corporate uniform most of them seem to wear, but I'm astounded so many are wearing the corporate colours and one or other of the inspirational slogans I've seen plastered on the walls.

Sweet Fucking Awesome!

Go For It!

Sweet Creative!

They are all written in a flowing script, in either purple or glowing multi-colours like a Dulux colour wheel, against the green of the T-shirt. They come in a variety of shorthand versions too; *Sweet FA. SFA, Sweet Fucking A, Fucking Sweet, GFI.*

How many of these people have kids, I wonder. Would I put on a T-shirt saying *Sweet Fucking Awesome* if I had a five-year-old? I imagine a Batman-suited toddler on a trike asking Daddy what SFA stands for. Have standards degenerated, or have I missed the evolution of language? I use the word *bloody* in front of my kids from time to time, if I hit my thumb with a hammer, or if the internet connection goes down. But it's not something I'm proud of. Yet I know Em thinks *fuck* is a mild emphasis to be used liberally with language like salt on chips. I muse that a T-shirt with *bloody fucking marvellous* on it might be in the marketer's pipeline.

I'm so busy reflecting on everybody's clothing choices that I miss the mention of my name.

"Jack?"

"Yes."

"It's you."

I hadn't noticed I'd been standing next to Carl, but he was now in my face gesticulating towards the front.

I hear, "Jack Cooper, are you in today?"

A few expectant faces are turned towards me and I realise the speaker is now a dark-haired woman in her thirties. She's calling me to the front, along with half a dozen new starters. I catch her eye and feel a slight tug in my stomach. She's attractive. A heart-shaped face framed by brunette hair cut into a shaggy bob. She's wearing a figure-hugging green T-shirt emblazoned with *Sweet FA* across her breasts and is beaming a smile that could light up a stadium.

She holds up a mobile phone and takes a video as I stumble through four or five rows of people to the front of the room. The new starters and me, stand in a self-conscious row staring out at the hundred or so faces. Only moments ago I had been inspecting the personalities in the room, making judgements and feeling superior. In a fleeting moment of inattention, the tables have turned and I'm the focus of a hundred pairs of eyes. I feel like I've just walked into an alien bar in Mos Eisley and the only thing missing is the music.

"Jack, welcome," says the woman.

I smile.

A picture of me appears on the TV screen. A live broadcast from the attractive woman's phone.

"Jack won an international prize at Imperial College

London for his software work on prototype compilers, and went on to lead the multi-national effort to build one of the very first graphical-based operating systems in the world."

I'm horrified to see the video tighten on my face.

She goes on: "Jack's credits include the earliest-known restful base architecture, way before the internet, and a distributed design for mission data used by the European Space Agency. But despite all these Sweet Fucking Awesome achievements …"

Pause for … *Yay. Jazz hands.*

"… his claim to fame is a score of seventeen thousand three hundred on *Space Invaders*. They used to call him Jack Magic."

Yay. Jazz hands.

"And I see you have a *Space Invaders* T-shirt on now, Jack."

The camera focuses on the T-shirt. The image is of the simple ten-point alien. Just one. Unmistakably, undeniably, perfectly a space invader. I didn't need to be reminded, but I look down anyway. I pull the shirt to make a display of it for everybody. What the fuck am I doing?

Everything she said was true. But where was she getting this stuff? It wasn't on my CV. "We are extremely lucky to have Jack join us; he's going to be running the Frozen Mammals team and we hope you love it here, Jack. Welcome."

Yay. Jazz hands.

Fucking embarrassing!

What she didn't say was that I'd been out of work for nine months, had remained as a software engineer for thirty years and never made it into management, had peaked on my earnings fifteen years ago and was now going down, hated working in software, hated technology and thought everybody in this *sweet fucking place* was a moron.

"Thanks," I say. I nod and smile.

With the pain of *All Cast* introductions over, I creep back up the stairs to my desk. I sit down and check emails. I'm already beginning to see a pattern. The Cast Champs seem to spend their days updating documents and sending out notifications: John has updated the *New Starters Pack*; Freya has edited the *All Cast Agenda*; Silas has reacted to Freya's comment on John's post about Friday's *Sweet Families* event. Thank fuck we have these people to run around commenting on each other's comments. I have no idea what the world did before email and instant messaging. Did business ever get done?

I read another message from my own Cast Champion, Freya. "Sorry to miss you this morning Jack. I hope everything is okay. I rescheduled for after the all cast meeting. I'll come and get you. :-)"

Oh boy! I'd hoped I could avoid contact with anybody for a while. And just as that thought is percolating through the gravel of my mind there's a knock on my desk and I look up to see the same dark-haired, attractive woman who introduced me to the group five minutes earlier.

"Hi, Jack. You ready for our chat?"

"Um." Though I think I actually said nothing, just opened my mouth a little to give my face a moronic, half-surprised, silent twat look.

Up close this woman is even more attractive than from a distance. I find myself staring at her like I might once have stared at Selina Scott on Breakfast TV. The difference being that Selina wasn't there in person and had no capacity to recoil at the adolescent attention, or indeed any way of knowing that a million teenage boys had pointless crushes on her. So sure, Selina had big-blonde eighties' hair with a centre parting and therefore the bonce styling bore no comparison to the spiky, dark-brown bob in front of me, but the elongated foxy face and wide mouth could have seen this modern woman present on *Breakfast Time* any day of the week.

Such instant attraction has happened to me before, and each time it's been accompanied by embarrassment at the stupidity of my own humanity and a bucket of guilt, because invariably I'd been in a relationship at the time. I had no reason to feel either of those emotions right now, but habits like this are ingrained in the brain from the earliest encounters with those you find sexually alluring.

I remember staring at my baked beans on toast for what seemed like hours when Katie Hedges came over for tea when I was nine. Unable to eat or talk, I listened as Mum asked questions about school, and Katie's netball team. Everything Katie said was wrapped in chocolate — not ordinary chocolate, but the chocolate they made Walnut Whips out of — that hid a sweet trove of sticky white revelation. I listened to every chocolatey word but was unable to add even half a walnut to the conversation. I may as well have been stuffed with sticky white revelation myself for all the use I was, and after that day I was so embarrassed I couldn't even approach her at school. She moved away that year, and my dreams of wild hide and seek in the playground were never realised.

Such moments make up the habitual mind paths that stay with us into our fifties and beyond, and right now the woman standing next to me was a Walnut Whip in all her seventies corner-shop glory.

"We had a catchup," she says.

Baked beans.

"I'm Freya."

Sticky white revelation.

"Your Cast Champ." She smiles, and must have decided the conversation was going to be one sided because she doesn't wait for me to reply. "I've booked a room downstairs. Shall we get a drink and take it down?"

I think I can sense dismay.

"Downstairs? Tea?" she says.

"Oh. Yeah." I finally manage to get some words out. They aren't my best, but at least there's something coming out of my mouth that makes a modicum of sense. "Yeah. Yeah. Tea's good."

I follow her across the mezzanine to the kitchen and we both make a drink. She asks some one-sided questions about how I'm getting on and have I got everything I need. I respond with ums and ahs, and — well, let's face it, thoughts of baked beans. Thank God the hot tea hits my stomach and I begin to take back some control from my primordial limbic system, which is currently running the show.

"Early days," I say. "I'm getting to know the team."

"They're awesome. Totally lit. You'll be fine. Man of your experience. They need that." She glances at my space invader and nods towards it. "Nice."

Baked beans.

I wonder what she's heard? Why did she say, *You'll be fine*? In what way am I in danger? Did I seem nervous? Of course, I did. Stupid. I couldn't string words together without thinking about a plate of baked beans or a Walnut Whip. I must be coming across like a turd, and not a dancing one.

We get to a large conference room and sit down at the central table already occupied by three others. New starters, apparently. Freya welcomes us, runs through a bit about the company and we take turns telling *Our Story* of how we came to be at Sweet and the pivotal moments of our careers. I list some bullet points on a sheet of A4 and read out a list of my jobs.

"Immense, Jack," Freya says. "Was there a really important realisation that meant you wanted to come and work here?"

The fact that there are others in the room stops me from diving into the usual self-pity about depression, separation, unemployment, estrangement, pointlessness and nihilism. They all look so expectant, confident, ready to receive my words as a reflection of who I am and what I believe in. How could I give them the truth? It would be like kicking a kitten, or telling your five-year-old that no matter how hard he tries he'll never be an astronaut or a sports star, that life is a winner-takes-all game and all the winners have been born to families of previous generations of winners and they aren't about to give you a spot on the podium. That would be *my* truth. Deep down. I could temper it and say something about being out of work for nearly a year, and that I desperately needed to get out of the flat before I drank myself into a kerbside grave on the last dregs of savings hidden in that ancient account I'd opened when I was a student because they gave me five quid for free. But that story wouldn't be optimistic either — to say the least.

So I say, "I've worked in engineering for a while, and I really wanted to get some experience in a vibrant commercial company. A firm that had a future in front of it using an exciting technology platform."

I can talk BS when I want to. I've learned I have to, to get through, I mean. It's like oil on the bicycle chain or keeping the code tidy when you're programming. If you don't, sooner or later things stop working. If you dare to be negative, people stop talking to you — you get sidelined. No matter your experience or knowledge of a topic, or how your words end up foretelling reality, you won't be asked to contribute because they feel you are always trampling over their sandcastles or sowing weeds in their flower beds. And I have a habit of pointing out the obvious. My wife tells me I'm nasty and destructive. Polarising. *Toxic* was the word she used, but I think she got it from a book. Yet, I wish I had learned much earlier in life to keep my mouth shut. But at least in my fifties, I think I've gained a little bit of wisdom. It's something.

Freya is looking at me with wide eyes. It's a bit unnerving, given how attractive she is. My gut twists. "That's awesome, Jack. You're an engineer, and you play *Space Invaders*," she says.

"Yes. Well, I've not played for a while. I can't remember the last time."

"I'll send you a link, you can impress us with your prowess."

I'm not sure if she's taking the piss or not. I check out her eyes for clues, but she seems genuine. Everybody is nodding and taking the comment seriously, too. It's weird. But I smile and say, "Sure, great."

She picks up her phone and within a few seconds I feel my own device vibrate in my pocket. I find it extraordinary how quickly digital natives can send messages. There must be some evolutionary process involved, because I can't even get through the security check in the time she's picked up her phone, found the information she needs and sent a link. It's amazing if you think about it. But I suppose if you did nothing else but play on a device for six hours a day from the age of three, you'd be good at it.

"Sent," she says. "I'll beat you any time you like."

Is she flirting? I can't quite work it out.

"You play *Space Invaders*?" I ask.

"My dad taught me. He was an engineer as well. We have some things in common."

She smiles and I have that stirring in my stomach again. Baked beans.

Freya gives us a presentation of the three company behaviours. And then she asks each of us what the behaviours mean to us personally.

Be Sweet Fucking Awesome. The finance guy beside me explains how this asks us to strive, to be our best and take care with everything we do.

Go for it. Apparently this phrase inspires us to take risks and be creative. Do first and ask permission later.

Sweet Creative. A call to out-of-the-box thinking. Don't get bogged down in the way it's always been done, find a new and better way.

I listen to the conversations. For a fleeting moment I'm caught up in the discussion and I find myself banging on about inspiration that comes when you have a shower and manage to solve a difficult problem. I could almost believe that had happened to me at some point in my life, but inside I know I'm paraphrasing Einstein or Archimedes or some other famous bloke that once wrote down his shower experience. But I see everybody nodding in agreement and encouraging me. They don't know I'm a fraud. They don't know I hate all this motivational stuff. What purpose does it achieve? Do we really think that people change their behaviour when they are given motivational statements on a pair of socks or a T-shirt? And if it does make a difference, is it more of a difference than if people just got on with their jobs and we eliminated an entire layer of motivational managers who seem to do nothing but promote inane

34

sayings and react to each other's reactions? I think not.

Freya talks us through the computer applications they use at Sweet. The usual stuff — email, word processors, spreadsheets, they use Google docs so everybody has access to everything by default.

And then she takes us in a new and utterly nonsensical direction.

"Who knows how to use the *rolling eyes* emoji?"

Silence.

She continues. "We use instant messaging so much at Sweet it can be overwhelming. But there are things you can do to help keep control of all the conversations going on. One of them is using the *rolling eyes*."

I roll my eyes. Metaphorically. Externally I'm smiling and nodding.

"When you get a Lazy IM from a colleague that's going to take a while to answer, just put in the *rolling eyes*. It means you're looking at it, but it doesn't start a whole new thread in the inbox."

I look around. I'm still in an office block in Berkshire. As far as I can tell, I haven't been teleported to Beijing by some fancy virtual reality technology. So why is this woman — albeit a damned attractive woman — talking in a language I can't understand? We're talking about colleagues who work in the same office building, probably at the next desk.

"Don't you just get off your chair and talk to them?" I ask. "Do we really need to know the official way of using the *rolling eyes?*"

She laughs and shakes her head. "It's not really official, Jack. But everybody's so busy that they prefer to use the *rolling eyes.*"

So busy curating their IM feeds, and finding *Sweet Creative* ways of using the application to avoid real work.

"When you've thought about the IM and are ready to answer," she says, "then it's okay to start a new thread. But the *rolling eyes* means you're taking their message seriously into consideration, you're thinking about it, and you're not ignoring it."

Thank fuck for that!

She explains the use of some other notable emojis. The *jazz hands* is used for applause or sometimes to say you volunteer for something, or also because you're happy about something somebody has said. *It's context based.*

So that means we've no fucking idea what anybody means by it.

She talks for several more minutes about how Sweet employees use the instant messaging system, IM for short. It's called Waste or Loose or Lazy or something. I've already forgotten by the time she gets thirty seconds in. But she shows us the application on a large TV screen and explains how to sort and search and manage the conversations.

"Every team has its own Lazy channel…"

That was it, *Lazy*.

"… and all the communities of practice and the guilds and the chapters…"

She's talking in tongues again.

"… and the workstreams and the projects. Channels pop up for all sorts of social events and there's one to welcome new Sweeties like yourselves."

Sweeties! How fucking awful is that.

"As soon as you get IM, Lazy, up and running, join the New Sweeties channel. It will help you get started. You can ask questions and find all sorts of useful documents and stuff you'll want to know in your first few months."

I feel sick. The long-term nature of this job dawns on me as she talks about needing a few months to get to grips with everything. And that's about right. From previous jobs I know it takes months to understand how truly fucking terrible a place is. First impressions start low and then, as you get to know the machinery, you can lower the bar even further while the cards house of optimism slowly collapses. That's work. That's life.

But she is very attractive.

Baked beans.

I get to my area and Vasi is the only team member sitting at a desk, so I check my watch. Two-thirty. Somehow I missed eating, but the team can't still be out?

"Is everybody still at lunch, Vasi?" I ask.

He — they — look up from the IM application they're busy tapping into. "Yeah. Maybe. Umm," they say. They look around the office, "Carl's on the sofa," and nod towards one of the many so-called breakout zones where Carl sits with his laptop. "I think Berry and Jinny might be vaping."

I imagine an enormous cloud of strawberry-smelling smoke on the pavement outside. "You going okay?"

Vasi points at his — I mean their/theys/its, select your fucking pronoun, cos I don't know — screen and says, "I'm really busy right now. Is it urgent that we talk?"

I'm stunned. I stare at them for a moment, uncertain how to proceed. I try a direct approach. "I need to know what everybody's doing. I am the manager."

"You're a squad master."

"Yeah. Squad master, manager, team leader. Take your pick."

"You don't manage. We can manage, thanks." They turn back to the screen and scroll up and down the IM channels.

There must be two hundred of them.

I could do one of several things here. I could shout at the little squirt and tell him that they and their pronoun confusion are fucking fired. But I suspect the only person leaving would be me. I could persist and nicely inform them that it is indeed urgent and I'd like their help finding out what everybody on Frozen Mammals is actually doing right now.

Or I could let it lie. Forget about the pronouns, breathe in and relax.

This is day two. I've been inducted into the cult of the *rolling eyes* and the *jazz hands* and that's probably more than enough for a Gen Xer to handle before teatime.

I decide to let it go for the day.

I get another cup of tea then sit down at my desk to figure out how to get on the New Sweeties channel. Perhaps that will tell me how to find my team.

3

On the way home I stop at *The Flying Pig*. There's just me and Larry and an old couple from out of town — well, I think they're from out of town. I've not seen them before. Larry's busy chatting them up and serving real customers instead of his usual mob of semi-drunks. I think he's enjoying the break, and I can hear him retelling the story of how he got the pub and how he'd always wanted to be a landlord and how when he retired from the airline, all he wanted to do was quietly sell a few pints to deserving working people in a rose-covered pub in the home counties. It's a lovely story, but his usual customers have heard it so many times he rarely gets the opportunity to bring it up.

I sit at the table nearest to the door and take out my mobile phone. I look at it. It's fully charged at the moment. That's quite a miracle, because recently I've been letting it run down so it doesn't bleep at me or tell me to update something. With the new job I want to be in touch in case anything happens. They haven't called yet, but I need to make it look as if I am in the modern world with the rest of them.

Larry arrives with my pint. He says, "You look tired, mate."

"Thanks. Four-hour values meeting this afternoon."

"What happened to just doing a job and getting paid for it?"

"I dunno. Madness," I say with a non-committal shrug.

I'm not in the mood for talking more and Larry senses the situation. He returns to the bar. Larry is always sensitive to the mood like that. It's comforting. He only gets involved when customers invite it. I'm told he has a baseball bat under the bar for when he needs to get really involved, but as a good publican he reads the room and lets his punters enjoy things at their own pace.

I flick through the news on the *Guardian* but find I don't bother reading to the bottom of the articles and get no satisfaction from the writing.

I launch Tinder. I'm nervous about it. It's part of what caused all the trouble with my marriage, but it's still there. I swear it talks to me during quiet moments, like a devil on my shoulder. As a nod to sensibilities, I've hidden it in a folder within a folder so my daughter doesn't find it.

I'm not a prostitute kind of guy. I never went to a prostitute as a young man. I found the idea unsavoury, wrong. But these days you can't avoid unsavoury things turning up in your life unless you unplug from the world. They come in twenty-four hours a day on the internet and in apps and emails and notifications. It's too easy. Until the internet, I had no idea where you went to find a prostitute. I imagined you cruised around dark parts of town and they turned up in your headlights, if you went slowly enough. Or perhaps you called one of those adverts in red telephone boxes and had a quick shag in the hedge just inside the park gates. Except, of course, there are no red telephone boxes anymore.

Then I heard that massage parlours gave out happy endings if you asked nicely. How do you ask? Is there a secret code? How do you ask without causing monstrous offence and labelling yourself as an embarrassment to mankind? I had no idea.

You see, by the time we broke up, the marriage hadn't been going well for a while. Since … well, since we moved home when the kids turned into teenagers, I guess — about ten years ago. That's not an excuse for my behaviour, I know, but it is a mitigation. Anyway, me and my ex managed to turn against each other and create years of fucking awful pain.

We shared the same space, but weren't together. Home life was a fucking great chore from seven in the morning until ten at night. Never a moment when I could be myself or me and Caroline could have some time together without something getting in the way. It was the kids, when they were young, of course — love 'em. The nappies, the nights, the feeds, the usual family-rending stuff that most of us are able to cope with. And then there's the next phase, when the little darlings start getting independent and opinionated and needing lifts and help and sandwiches and treats and … and … and …

But we found the most difficult time was reconciling my expectations of family life with what the kids actually wanted to do — which was mostly to sit on their beds playing games on some device or other (I think I might have mentioned this). Every tiny request became a point of conflict. I'd want to weed the paths, so I'd ask the kids for help; they'd be rude while refusing. I'd retaliate with wireless downtime, they'd get furious, Caroline would overrule me and then *I'd* get furious and kick off. It was a never-ending pattern.

Both of us were in pain, extended pain, and we blamed each other. But I think it was her fault. She had an affair because the opportunity presented itself on the internet — delivered by wireless device.

Caroline enabled the destabilising impact of the internet.

After uni, she went into teaching and the job slowly evolved from a career of autonomy and craft to one of box ticking and direction from above.

Even a move into the private sector didn't insulate her from change. Private schools, and hers in particular, had the resources to embrace the *advances* of digital connections. They scheduled video lectures from eminent scientists in the US, held discussion groups in email chat rooms, and encouraged social media connections to schools in Asia and South America. You couldn't deny the opportunities technology was bringing.

But I remember the fateful conversation.

We are making dinner. It's some kind of vegetable curry and I spill curry powder on the workbench.

"Nice! You turning into an old man?" Caroline says.

I think she's joking, but detect a rasping edge to her comment and I know she's had a bad day. But hey, nobody deliberately spills curry powder. It's not the sort of thing you want to clean up; it leaves yellow stains on the bench, and the dishcloth needs profuse rinsing to get rid of the turmeric. And then your hands smell. Besides, I'd had a bad day too, she didn't have a monopoly on moods, men are allowed to be moody.

"Fuck off." I leap straight in with the ten-megaton MAD reaction. It's wrong. I know it's wrong. She knows it's wrong. We both know it's not even meant like it sounds. It's so ridiculously over the top for the context that it can't possibly be serious. But it's an opening shot and it says, *If you want to argue, I can argue. Don't mess unless you're gonna push it to the max.*

She looks at me, shocked.

She has two choices. First, she can back down and take it as the overreaction it is. She can say something like, *Oooh!*

Did somebody press your alt-shift-delete keys today? And I would respond with, *Sorry, I'm a bit grumpy and turmeric really gets up my nose.* Then we'd carry on with dinner, it would be tasty and filling, but otherwise unremarkable, and then we'd settle down for the evening; her on her laptop, the kids on their tablets and me trying to get everybody to engage with a movie or some documentary on BBC2, or dare to suggest we play a board game or have a conversation, or bring up the decorating that still needs to be done.

Or she could make the second choice. She could pick up the venom stick and beat me with it. She would start with, *You fucking arsehole, how dare you say that to me,* and we would shout insults at each other. I would call her a fucking control freak and she would say I was a boring twat. And so it would go on until one of us stormed out of the kitchen. Maybe I would go down the pub or she would go and visit her girlfriends, or perhaps both.

Then maybe, just maybe, we'd meet up in the middle of the bed at midnight and cuddle, or maybe we'd cuddle in the morning. But whichever cuddle schedule we chose, by the next evening we'd be back in the kitchen cooking chilli or bolognese and it would be her turn to drop something.

We'd been in this place before.

I had given her options.

I wait for her to make the choice.

Caroline knows all about me. She knows I have struggled and feel worthless. She tried to support me and stick with me as I faced a crisis in my mid-life.

So presented with the MAD option, she doesn't scream at me to pull my head out of my arse. She doesn't crack a joke. She doesn't try to make light of it.

She takes neither expected option.

She calmly picks up the dishcloth from the stainless-steel

rack by the sink, rinses it, walks to the spilt curry powder and begins to wipe it away.

And then she says, "I'm having an affair. He's called Mark. I met him on an internet conference call."

I watch her clean the yellow powder off the work surface using her hand as a scoop. She doesn't look at me. She moves slowly, deliberately, like you might if you were trying to take one of the last few moves in Jenga before the tower collapses. I feel a sickness in my throat like a punch to the chest but with no physical force, just the weight of words contained in a life-threatening revelation put across in a mundane announcement to match the mundanity of her lover's name. Mark.

When she takes the spilt powder over to the sink and rinses the cloth, she finally looks at me. I must be looking puzzled, and I know I'm thinking this might be a sick joke, but she nods. She confirms.

Just like that, with a nod, I learn the one single fact in my mid-life that will now define the next part of my fleeting existence on Earth. More than rising sea levels, robotic drones, Brexit, Trump, the alt-right and massacres in — I don't know, take your pick — Syria, Myanmar, Ukraine, Thousand Oaks, New Zealand. More than any of these massive events, a simple nod destroys one personal reality and ushers in a new, more frightening future.

So I'm sitting in the pub with Larry's story going on by the bar and with Tinder in front of me, and my thoughts are with my family and Caroline. Because, with all that explanation for the breakup of my marriage and laying the blame at the door of my wife's affair and the loneliness of modern family life, I have missed the single most damaging part of the story because it is still hard to admit. It still hurts that I grew into, and still am, a person I don't understand

and don't like. It is a hard fact that a year before Caroline found love online in a video chat room, I had been sneaking off to prostitutes I contacted through another online app, Tinder. I pay to play.

What I didn't know then, was that my wife had known this all along.

4

Em is in my room at 7:30 a.m. shaking me awake.

"Come on, Dad. Time to get ready for work. Here's a coffee. I'll make you some breakfast."

I hear her put a mug of coffee on the bedside table and walk to the window. She opens the curtains. "It's a shitty day," she says.

No kidding. *Every* day is shitty. I hear her soft footsteps go into the kitchen. She bangs a couple of cupboard doors and the fridge. I open my eyes and see the 'World's Greatest Dad' mug next to the bed. It steams a little; the heating's not on yet.

But I'm not the world's greatest. Not by a long way.

Sleep is escape, and waking like a prison. I manage to pull myself up and reach for the coffee. I take a sip. Em's put sugar in and it's nice and milky, just how I like my first coffee of the day. I smile, but as I drink, the previous evening's events play back in my mind and I'm flooded by a deep shame that starts in my stomach and rises round my torso, up my neck until the hairs on the back of my head feel like they are standing up.

Her name was Mandy. She must have been twenty-two or twenty-three. A student, she said, making money for her Masters, but who knows. We met in a bar and she took me in an Uber to her place. We had sex. I paid 120 quid. It was a transaction, nothing more. The whole thing lasted less than an hour, and for that hour I was away from everything else. I'd not met her before, but I'd seen her profile on

47

Tinder clearly marked as 'pay to play'. She was my daughter's age.

She had a curvy, full body and a rich growth of dark pubic hair.

She was my daughter's age.

Jesus Christ.

"Eggs or porridge?" Em asks from the door. "Don't you think you need to be getting into the shower?"

"Yeah, give me a moment. You let yourself in this time?"

"I thought you might need some encouragement."

"Yeah," I say to myself.

"Eggs or porridge, then?"

"Eggs. Thanks, sweetheart."

I take a glug more coffee and slide out of bed. I shower, get dressed, and when I get into the kitchen Em has prepared scrambled eggs on toast with orange juice.

"You bought me juice," I say.

"I am full of wonders."

"Yes. How's work going?"

Em works for an NGO campaigning for 'climate action'. It's her dream job, and she picked it up straight out of college. For Em, a plastic carton of orange juice is not just orange juice. It's air miles, rampant consumerism, reckless agricultural practices, thoughtless packaging, inadequate government intervention, slave labour, feeble consumer choices, poor legal protection and a whole peel of other issues I can't begin to be concerned about. For her to buy me a carton to support me in my new job borders on betrayal of her values. It took a lot. I'm touched.

"It's good. But don't go thinking I've gone soft, Dad. I paid over and above for the carbon offset on that orange juice."

I smile. "Well, it tastes good."

"Don't start."

No. I shouldn't. And anyway, I agree with her. I just don't have the energy to fight for what's right like she does.

"How was yesterday, Dad? You going to like working for a funky company?"

Is that what it is? Sweet Funky Awesome. I shrug. "You know. It's a job. It'll be okay."

"Dad?" Her simple word comes out with a serious undertone, like when I used to call the children's names just before they drew on the wall with a crayon or put a knife in their mouth. "Dad, I want to ask you a favour."

"Of course, anything you want."

"No, not like that. Not easy stuff. It's different." She takes a drink from her coffee. She looks around the kitchen and sighs.

"Well. Yes. Of course. If I can do it. What is it?" I'm beginning to grow fearful. Em has tried to get me and Caroline back together before, and she's not beyond manipulation when it comes to getting what she wants. She's arranged for us to both show up at the same bar together and has sent gifts labelled from each other. She's devious.

"I've got everything I need except for one thing, and I think it's something that's going to be very hard for you?"

"Look, if it's getting back with your mother, we've talked about it before. She doesn't want me and doesn't deserve me. I don't want to hurt her anymore." Caroline has gone through her own cycle of therapy and SSRI experimentation in the last few years. I don't think she'd have me back if I turned into Ryan Gosling with Brad Pitt's haircut.

"No, Dad. It's not that. It's just about you."

"Well?" I push some egg around the plate for a bit,

waiting for her to speak.

"I want you to make a go of this new job. You need to work …" She wells up but keeps talking as her eyes first glaze with tears and then drops form on her lower lids. "You need something to focus on, to do during the day to keep you healthy. Dad, you're wasting away and I'm worried you're going to die."

To see your child express fear for your future is heartbreaking. It's heartbreaking because you both know that life doesn't go on forever, and that one day you will be separated. But it's also heartbreaking because the gravity of the parent-child relationship is set out naked in front of you both as if the elephant in the room has finally been noticed and comes to sit at the table. It's a relationship so heavy with interdependence that we have to ignore it in case our close attention damages it in some way, or it disappears. We are all reliant on our relationships with our parents for good and for bad. We are the product of these relationships, and it's been this way for half a million years. Probably more.

I reach over the table and take Em's hand. "I'm not going anywhere."

She looks up, defiant even as tears trickle down her cheeks. "You say that but you're getting worse. If I hadn't come round, you'd have missed another morning. You can't start a job like this, Dad. Did you intend to get up for work?"

I take my hand back and look down at the cooling eggs. "Yes," I say. But I hadn't. I'd have slept in, nursing the shame of my late-night encounter with Mandy and a blistering headache from the beer. I'd have called in sick and gone to the pub at lunchtime for a sharpener. I'd have wasted the day and probably found myself watching TV into the night with a curry or kebab, ready to miss tomorrow too.

"I don't think I can get on there. They're so young. I don't understand them. They don't seem to do any work."

"They do, Dad, they just do it their way."

I scoff. "Ha, I don't see any evidence."

She raises her voice a bit. "You have to give it a try," and then a bit more, "Do it for me?" She's welling up again. She wipes her eyes. "You don't have to fit in, you just have to be you. They'll accept you. It's what we do. We accept people. All people."

"So I can be just fucking normal. Boring. An old fuck up."

"No. You're you, Dad. Don't be like this … it's …" She cups her hands to her face. "Dad. Take back your life," she whispers into her hands.

This is pain. Sickening pain. It's the pain of the curry powder moment. Pain like when my own father died. Pain as physical as if a thug with a baseball bat was dishing out whacks to the stomach.

"I don't think I can," I say.

"I'm asking this for me and for you. This is serious. I'm serious."

I shake my head. "The job's not for me."

"What is, Dad? What is for you then? Tell me. What job are you going to do?"

"Not this."

The tears are suddenly gone. She's staring at me. I've seen this look before, it's what she wears when something gruelling has to be done but she's made the decision to see it through. And she always does. It's one of the qualities of Em I love above all else. I think she gets it from her mother, because it's certainly not from me. Whatever she puts her mind to, she completes it.

51

"Then we're done," she says.

"What?"

"Finished," she says. "I'm not your daughter. I'm nobody to you." She stands up violently. The chair crashes to the floor behind her. She runs for the door.

"Em. No. Don't do this. It's crazy."

"You're doing it, not me. Goodbye, Dad."

She's gone.

I sit for a long while staring towards the window watching the rain smash on the pane and the black clouds race across the sky. I could feel free now to do what I want. Abandon the new job, sit in the house or go to the pub, no mothering daughter can tell me what I should or shouldn't do. I mean, what right did she have anyway?

But I feel empty. Yeah, so that's a cliché, feeling empty, lost, numb, all those things, yet those are the best words I can come up with to describe how I feel. While I feel those things, though, I'm also analysing my next actions and what they would mean now I've been asked to make a go of the job and have refused.

If I now go to work, am I giving in to pressure? Would I be a slave to my daughter's demand? Or would I, in fact, be asserting my right to go to work? And if I make the decision to go to work, should I call my daughter and tell her I've changed my mind, or have I simply carried on as if she never asked me and therefore she has no need to know.

And what if I don't go to work? What if I go down the pub and ask Larry to pour me a pint of his best IPA and get blind drunk before lunchtime? Would that mean I'd changed my day because of my daughter's request, and therefore done it just to spite her? To show her who was in control of my life. But then again, because I'd changed my day to spite her, wouldn't that mean I wasn't actually in control, that external factors were controlling me and I was, whichever way you looked at it, blowing in the wind of my daughter's request? Jesus. It's enough to do your head in.

And at the back of this ridiculous train of thought is the fear that I am not, and never have been, in control of my own actions. They are always actions as a result of some external factor or other. Can anybody truly say they act independently and would do what they do regardless of what else was going on? Somebody who says they do their job for the love of it … would they really do that job if everybody in the world suddenly stopped paying them any attention? I doubt it.

So where the fuck does that get me? Whatever I do, I am somebody's puppet. I am not myself. I am a shell of a man living in a single-bed flat with a drink and whore addiction.

I look at the kitchen clock. It's coming up for 8 a.m.

And then the doorbell goes. I don't want to see anybody. I ignore it.

The doorbell goes again and I hear a shout from the road. "Jack. Open the door. It's me?"

Caroline.

I'll pretend I've gone out.

"I know you're there," she shouts.

How? She can't know unless she's been out there with Em.

Oh, fuck. Of course. She's been out there with Em. This whole thing is a plot.

"Buzz me in, Jack." The doorbell goes again, and again and again.

Then the bell goes quiet and I hear footsteps coming up the stairs followed by thumping on the door. Somebody must have let her in.

"Open up, Jack."

I can't escape. It's a pincer movement. I open the door and she stands framed by the architraves.

"What the fuck?" she says.

"You look nice."

"Piss off. What the fuck have you done to our daughter?"

I sigh. "Can you leave me alone. I'm really not in the mood."

"Not in the mood," she mocks with a child's voice. Then adds, "You can't fucking hide, you coward. Not this time. Not with this."

I don't know what she means, but she walks past me to the table. She sits down. I watch, holding the door open in the vain hope she'll turn around and go back out.

"Come and sit down," she says.

I close the door.

She's calmer. Conciliatory.

I pick up the chair Em knocked over and sit down. Caroline's soaking wet from the rain and it's flattened her hair. Her eye makeup is running. But she does look nice. Soft.

"You do look nice," I say. I grimace inside. I can't stop myself.

She sighs and shakes her head.

"Jack," she says, "it's time to stop fucking your life up. Time to sort yourself out and become a man."

"A man like Mark, I suppose?"

"Fuck off. No. Not a man like Mark. A man like Jack. Like you. Like you used to be when I met you. You were so full of ideas and passion. You were going to build machines to make life better for the world, programs that sent us to other planets. You had ideas that seemed like fantasy but which have all come true. But you've not been involved in making that happen. Why not? What has happened to you? You can't even keep a job for a fucking day."

I stay silent. But my thoughts race. Really. I don't know. I don't know how to explain it. "We've been over all this. You know. It's all so pointless."

She sighs. "It's not pointless."

She's wrong. Honestly, I've spent years on things that I thought were important and were suddenly cancelled. A week later I'd be working for another company or on another project. I worked on amazing concepts that never saw the outside of a lab. And those things that did come into the daylight, ostensibly to make things simpler and easier, and more controllable and clearer, usually had exactly the opposite effect. I was working for the sake of pushing products out the door, not improving anything except the bank balances of the shareholders — and that's if it wasn't frittered away on executive sales trips or bonuses.

And when I look at all the computer things I've bought over the years I realise I've been part of the big wheel. Turning my head from perfectly good ideas towards the new shiny toy, handing over thousands of pounds and getting nothing except another thing to fix when it didn't work as advertised or didn't work with that application or didn't work unless you downloaded a new driver or registered for this account or that app needed updating and had you checked your virus signatures and where did my emails go and why has it lost my document and where the fuck did the download go and why is the wireless so slow and can we upgrade the bandwidth and …

I'm breathing heavily and staring out of the window.

"Are you going to even talk to me?" she says.

I look at her. But I'm not about to admit any of my crazy

thought processes to her on a rainy Wednesday morning when my daughter has tried to bully me into changing my attitude and Caroline has thundered up the stairs to put the boot in.

"Jack. Talk to me."

I go on the offensive. "Did you hatch this little plan by yourself, or was it both you and Em?"

She closes her eyes. When she opens them she's staring at the floor.

She doesn't respond so I pick up where I left off. "We're separated now, in case you've forgotten. You don't get to control me anymore," I say, as viciously as I can muster.

"Jack."

"And I can't believe you roped Em into your scheme. It's pathetic." I hear myself as if somebody else is talking. As if I'm looking on from the sofa at some old married couple warring over warming the teapot. And from where I sit, it's clear I'm the one in the wrong. I know that it's me that must change. I know that Caroline is behaving like an adult and I'm the child. But I only see that from the sofa. Not when I inhabit the body, if you see what I mean.

"Jack. Nobody controls you. You are pathetic by your own choice."

"I'm pathetic?"

"You don't shave. You don't look after your body, you don't pay attention to anybody. You've barely worked at anything and when you have, you've found some reason to be sacked or to resign. And you've—" She stops and stares at me like the next words are too hard to say.

"Go on. Say it again." I know what she's thinking. I start shouting. "Go on. Bang on about Tinder again, completely forget about your fucking video conference lover. Blame me for fucking everything like the pathetic man I am in your perfect fucking eyes."

She's shouting over me now. Something about it not being her fault and it's not about us anyway, it's about the children now and the new baby or something. She is fucking fierce. She doesn't quite start bashing the table or throwing things — not this time — but as she shouts, I carry on with my own agonising attack, which is really just a smokescreen to stop us talking about me. I shout about how her affair fucked up any chance we had, and what sort of role model was she for Em, and what did our son make of her. No wonder he turned out so fucked up. "You're a fucking slapper."

She stops shouting.

I stop shouting.

She's horrified. Disgusted.

So am I.

She's sobbing into her hands. "Don't bring Geronimo into this."

"Don't call him that. His name is Oscar." I say it quietly with bitterness. I'm in control.

"Jack. Jack. Please. Get over it."

"Get over it? It's ruined everything."

"Not that. Not now, Jack. Please. I have something else to say."

In a moment of quiet, I take a deep breath. "What else do you have to say?"

"Jack," she says into her hands. "Just listen to me, Jack. Just fucking listen for a moment. This isn't about you or Geronimo."

I'm quiet. I'm listening.

"Em's pregnant. She needs you."

I sit back in my chair. I fold my arms. I don't want to hear this. But I must.

"She's not asking you to go to work for your sake. It's not to make *you* happy. *You* don't *have* to be happy. She's asking for her baby. She wants her daddy back, and she wants her child to have a grandfather."

I met Caroline when we were at university. She studied mathematics at Imperial while I studied engineering. And I mean studied. Neither of us used university as a social club, like so many of the stories you hear. For us it was work — because actually, the study was the play, and the play was the study. For me the beauty of experimentation and resolution, the empirical method, was like spending time with Archimedes himself. Days in a state of wonder and awe. And for her, the symmetry and perfection you could get from an equation or proof shadowed anything else you could be doing with your time.

Almost. Because while we studied, we also fucked beautifully. In total contrast to the mental worlds we inhabited during the days and early evenings, at night our animal bodies took over, driven by deep prehistoric synapses. We did it like they do on the Discovery Channel.

So I can't help thinking about that when Caroline gives me a peck on the cheek just before she leaves a couple of hours later. It's tender. Loving, almost. She whispers, "We're going to be grandparents. I know you'll be fine." The whisper warms my ear. I miss her.

We both agree to be good grandparents. We both agree to support and love Em through this, unexpected but … well, it's life affirming, really.

I close the door behind her and I begin to cry as if I'm adding to the rain. The tears are of those happy-sad sort. The ones that lament the past while being hopeful about the future.

I put on some shoes, a raincoat and take the short

collapsible umbrella I keep hanging on the back of the door. I don't yet know where I'm going, but as I walk through the puddles and listen to the cars splash water onto the pavement and the rain splatter on the umbrella above my head, I find that step by step, I'm drawn to Sweet's offices and my new position as team leader, or squad master or member of the cast, or frankly whatever ridiculous role they make up.

Because I've decided.

I'm going to do it.

Because if I don't, I will be failing myself, and crucially, I will be failing a blameless life that deserves a functioning, loving grandfather.

5

I get to my desk and my team aren't there. People I haven't been introduced to are milling about, but the office seems quiet compared to the days before. I don't mind. I have things to do.

I first take out my phone and tap in the PIN. I have some messages from Em from a few days before; one from Em from this morning saying she was on her way over. I have a — what do you call a collection of text messages from one place that you don't want? A binload? A rubbish of? Anyway, they are from Vodafone to say I have a bill to pay, or there's a new voicemail, or would you like a Wonderful Wednesday offer of unlimited texts to the moon or Jupiter or something. I delete them all. This is to be a new start in my relationship with the phone.

I don't think. I do.

I delete Tinder. It's gone. It takes a second. I feel clean, and I'm surprised that the delete app worked. I'm not used to things on my phone actually working first time, especially when it's in the interests of the makers of such apps to have them fail to delete themselves.

But it really has gone.

When Caroline nodded confirmation of her affair with video-con-attendee Mark, the marriage went from bad to fucked-up-beyond-all-reasoning. Up to that point we had both lived in some sort of strange aether world where the truth of our marriage collapse had failed to manifest; as we moved about the house and went to work and

61

accomplished the daily chores, we somehow managed to avoid reality. We made breakfast, put the rubbish out, helped the kids with their stuff, watched TV, drank beer and wine. For months. But she knew I'd got Tinder on my phone and had used it to organise a couple of evening fucks with young women. Three or four fucks, actually. Four.

She found out because she suspected something was up and installed a tracking app on the phone. She followed me to a block of flats well known for its night-time services. I didn't know. I thought it was this particular young woman's flat, not a brothel. But Caroline knew. Or found out. And then she said nothing for weeks and let me carry on cleaning dishes and making curry as if nothing had changed.

But of course it had changed.

It had changed before she found out. It changed the moment the opportunity arrived by way of a picture on an app on a phone over the internet. And then it changed further when my wife viewed a movie on a screen via an app, delivered over the internet. Irrevocable damage done in a way that had been impossible ten years earlier. I'm angry because neither of us asked for these opportunities to turn up just when we were most vulnerable. Just when I was wading through the mud of a mid-life crisis, feeling useless because my kids were growing up wrong, and just when she was at the end of her compassion for me. Sin can be hard to resist at the best of times, but when you are grubbing through the weeds of your life in search of a path out of the garden, it's impossible to avoid an easy distraction from the undergrowth that promises excitement for a few hours. It's hard to be faithful when nobody is selling virtue and everybody is selling sin.

I realise I sound like some born-again nutter, but it's useful for me to put it in these terms. There are normal things that we want to mostly be like. Most of us want to be stable and sensible and conscientious and, well, normal — boring, if you like. What are we doing if we make it easier and easier to behave selfishly and thoughtlessly? If even the dull and boring among us are able to act as hedonistic eccentrics? We are gnawing at the bones of civilisation.

But now Tinder is gone. I have made one small concession to stop gnawing and to build.

Because during my walk through the rain I made some resolutions. First I resolved to delete Tinder. Done. Next I resolved to embed myself into the people and technologies at Sweet. I would be optimistic and encouraging. I would be Sweet Fucking Awesome, a model Sweetie. Then I resolved to give up drinking except in social situations at work, where I seriously doubted I'd be able to avoid alcohol. And finally I resolved to take on the zoomers and the millennials at their own game. I would show the little fuckers how to use technology. I would not only understand the rolling eyes, I would learn all the acronyms and cool words. I would be unafraid of pronouns, PC language and silly alt-corporate speak. I would do it first. And then I would become it.

Filled with enthusiasm for my new life, I open my laptop and press the black button to get it fired up.

Updating.

I wait.

Updating.

FFS.

I look around. A few people are congregating in the kitchen, but there's still no sign of my team.

"Jack?"

"Yes." I look up. It's my direct manager. I met him for a half-hour interview just after Amber spoke to me. I think he's called Ted. I'm not sure, and I hope that's not written all over my face. He's high up in Sweet but honestly I've forgotten how high, I don't pay attention to that sort of thing. I just know he's a step or two above me on the ladder and that puts him on the board somewhere. I don't believe all that nonsense about flat hierarchies and accessible managers. Underneath, they are the same status-driven individuals they always were. Companies can be as flat as they like on paper, while the reality will always be a human construct of petty jealousies and power struggles.

Yes, he's called Ted. He's got a friendly smile.

We exchange the usual, clichéd moments of such things. He asks how my first few days have been and I reply that it's going well and there's a lot to take in. He says something about the hardworking enthusiastic staff and I nod in approval. It's pointless from an information-gathering perspective, but it's the first manoeuvre in what will be a several-years-long relationship. I've never heard of a business manager opening the conversation with a new member of staff with something like, "Looking sharp today, Jack," or even, "How did the prostate check go? That new doctor has really stubby fingers." We, as human beings, don't like it very much when people are over familiar.

So, I'm surprised when he says, "How's Caroline?"

A few possibilities and questions whizz through my mind, like a swarm of asteroids on the edge of the screen that you don't want to commit to shooting yet because they will just break up into more and smaller questions.

But in the end I plump for, "She's well. I didn't realise you knew her," even though I know this will inevitably lead to a conversation and the slow reveal of an unknown history.

He looks down at me. I feel uncomfortable. He might be

too close to my personal space or too tall — he's at least six-two — or maybe it's because I should remember him but don't, and I'm feeling the beginning of a rush of embarrassment.

He's bald. Well, he's lost the hair on top and the rest is shaved so close it's more like stubble. I guess he's a few years younger than me, in his mid-forties, and there's something familiar about his eyes and his dark eyelashes. But I can't place him.

"Well, I don't know her well. I met her once when you and I worked at Fergusons."

"You worked at Fergusons?"

"Yes." He pauses and looks a bit self-conscious. It's not the sort of expression I expect from a manager. Like most managers in computer-type companies, he's taller than most of the workers. This is a clear and observable fact. Not that *he's* taller, but that most male managers are taller. In some places I've worked, the height of the senior managers is an embarrassment. I feel sure that if owners of companies read the evidence showing the positive discrimination in favour of tall men, they would quickly change their thinking, just so it didn't look as if they were stupid. So, given that he's tall and in IT, the self-consciousness is something of a surprise. I'd normally expect false confidence, jumping to conclusions and solutions, and making decisions without displaying full knowledge of the situation.

"I was in the testing area. Quality manager." He pulls up a chair and sits. "Erm … I was sacked. You might remember." He pulls a toothy grin.

I think back to my time at Fergusons. "Edward?"

"Yep. That's me." He smiles. "I use Ted, now. Just in case I run into anybody from the past."

I start laughing.

"I thought you might have realised," he says.

"No. I didn't. Sorry. I haven't seen anybody from that era for years." I think for a moment.

Ted waits.

"And you had hair to your shoulders," I say.

"Yes. I couldn't keep it. It fell out." He rubs his baldness.

"Lawrence? You remember? He was delivery manager," I say. "A bit older than us. I went to his retirement party a few years back. I kept in touch somehow."

"Married a Singaporean woman. His third marriage, if I remember. What was her name?"

"Tzu. He met her on the internet. One of the first internet brides."

Ted smiled. "It's common these days."

"Common? I think it's obligatory."

Ted nods. "Caroline is your wife's name, isn't it?"

"Was," I say. And then to clarify, I add, "We separated."

"Sorry to hear."

"Shit happens."

I look around the office. It's just me and Ted. I move in a bit closer and speak softly. "You were sacked for painting a giant penis on the managing director's door?"

Ted laughs. "That's about the size of it." He stretches his arms out wide.

"I remember it being bigger than that. The entire company was in shock."

"The MD nearly burst a vein in his temple he was so furious. His face went purple and he jumped up and down like a giant pickled beetroot."

There was laughter, in private, but in those shirt, tie and suit days most of us were appalled. It was beyond comprehension, and Ted had been marched off the premises by security. No one was ever told why the quality manager had suddenly turned on the MD.

I ask, "What happened? We never knew why you did it."

"Simple. He refused to give me parental leave after the birth of my first child. Said I was too important to the company. There was some big European order going on at the time, and I was indispensable." He makes air quotes as he says indispensable.

"Yeah, that's right. We fucked it up. Promised too much and delivered too little." I shake my head.

"Such irony."

"Beautiful for you?"

"You could say. I found it difficult to get a job for a while after that."

I nod. No kidding.

There's a moment of quiet. I'm thinking about the injustice of it all and how parental leave couldn't possibly be refused anymore. How nowadays it would be the MD that would be sacked or held to account by some sort of hashtag movement that would turn the internet to fury.

Ted's looking at my desk, at the laptop that's still updating, and around the area at the empty desks. "You working okay with your team?" he asks.

I'm not sure what to say. *Lazy fuckers who are never here*, springs to mind, but I catch myself, even though it's turned out we have a surprise shared past. I remember my commitment to keeping the job. "Getting to know them. Finding out about the work. You know." It's back to the usual talking-to-the-boss bullshit. I add, "I think you've grown a great culture here," and I try to make it sound as sincere as I can.

Ted nods but doesn't say anything. In fact he looks disgruntled. "And your computer's set up okay?" He nods towards the little spinning thing in the middle of the screen.

"Updating." I shrug.

Then I can't help having a moan. It just comes out. "It's done something I didn't ask for, probably don't want, I can't possibly know about and it's done it when I needed to check my emails."

Ted starts laughing, which encourages me.

"I need another device for when one of them is updating and I need to check essential information. Maybe I need a tablet in case both update at the same time. You remember, don't you? It never used to be this way, because updating things was so hard. You needed to go back to the shop or send for something by mail order. Now it's so easy to update we're forced to do it all the time."

"Our app does that," says Ted. He's smiling, and laughing, but he's also sad.

His confession shuts me up briefly, but because I really do loathe updating I can't stop myself from saying, "It's another one of those advances I don't think anybody would vote for if they got the chance. I mean, it was sort of interesting when the first apps went online to update, but it's a nightmare now everything you own wants a piece of your time. I have apps that telephone to ask to be updated and apps that hang on like ghosts even after they've been deleted." I give it my best air quotes. "'I've noticed you've uninstalled Slippery-snake. Were you unhappy with the service. Here's a special two-month reduced rate if you install the latest version in the next 24 hours.' And then a day later you get a text to ask if you missed the first text. It's got out of control."

Ted's laughing hard. It takes him a moment to catch his breath. "That's hilarious."

I think he's serious. But I'm embarrassed that I've displayed a bit too much of the old-fucker.

Then he looks at his phone. He says, "I gotta go. Let me know if there's anything I can do. I think you'll be good in this role. Take your time. Get in easy. We'll talk."

"Sure," I say. I'm not certain what I'm saying "sure" to. I think I might be missing a subtext, but Ted has clearly made up his mind that the conversation about giant penises daubed on office doors and my hatred of inappropriate updates has run its course. "Sure," just seems like sensible response.

The laptop has finally got online and I start looking for the website to install the IM Lazy app on my phone. I figure I'm going to need to be better informed around here.

Turns out my team are in some planning meeting; I find out from the IM Lazy app. I should be in there too. I gather a pen and paper from the printer nearby and head down to Pulp Fiction — a room that seats ten people, according to the appointment. At last I expect to find out what the team is working on and how I might help. I've had an induction into the culture, a tutorial on the use of rolling eyes, lessons on how the IM is to be used and a lecture on modern pronoun use, but I have yet to understand what it is the team do.

Sweet builds an app called Sweet. It's a sort of bank account and budgeting tool all rolled into one, so you can set individual limits on the type of spending you make and then track your payments. You can even ask it to block certain types of purchases, and that's useful for stopping your kids buying alcohol and making sure you stick to your budgets. I've never used it, but I gather the idea is that it gives you back control of your finances.

Taking back control is a very popular thing to be doing these days. The company started in New Zealand a few years ago, was purchased by a UK company, brought over here, and is suddenly everywhere — worldwide, it seems — in the space of a few months. Sweet clips the ticket on every transaction that goes through and it charges a subscription. As I understand it, Sweet is making a shitload of money. *Sweet Fucking Awesome. Yay! Jazz hands.*

I sit through the planning sessions listening to the kids work out what they want to do in the next couple of weeks. I ask a few questions when I don't understand, but mostly I keep quiet and, quaintly, make a few notes on the sheets of paper I have with me. Everybody else has a laptop in front of them; they tap away endlessly. I am desperate to know if they are typing about work or sending each other instant messages.

"I want to work on improving the payment processing," says Carl. "It's a right mess at the moment and I reckon we can make it work much better with far fewer lines of code."

"Yep. And I can take the internationalisation of the accounts page. That will be fun," says Vasi.

One by one they discuss and dish out the work according to their personal preferences.

I'm puzzled. I say, "What's the goal here? What do you want to achieve?"

They look bemused.

"I mean, who decides what's most important?"

"We do, in here," says Carl.

I try to shake the image of him pole dancing in a g-string.

"We'll help you," he says. "You've not been a squad master before?"

It's true. I've not been a squad master. But this seems a hit-and-miss approach to dishing out work.

"You are, like, the guardian of the culture," Carl adds. "You make sure we don't blame each other for things that go wrong, spend plenty of time talking about our values and behaviours, and how that makes us feel—"

"And making sure we treat each other like humans," adds Vasi.

I wonder if what they think my job is, is what my job is. It's not what I signed up for, but who can argue with a team working for one of the fastest-growing and most successful medium-sized businesses in the country. They must be doing something right.

They are not collectively a group to which I wish to belong. Ginny spends much of her time swapping between her laptop and her phone. Her lack of attention is accepted by the group uncritically and with ease. She is the worst offender, but the others are by no means focused on the discussions that grow organically from some comment or other, take in a bit of searching online and perhaps the dredging up of a document, and fizzle out as everybody returns to their phones or their laptops. A few minutes of silence might go by and then another comment will set the cycle going again.

I watch this go around a few times then I say, "Okay, how about some actions out of the meeting?"

"We do everything face to face or on Lazy if we need to keep a record," says Carl. "You'll get used to us." He smiles, and adds after he looks round the table, "We're a tight team. *Yay!*" He weaves his fingers together in a sort of basket in front of his face and judders them about. I take this to signify the tightness he's talking about, but it could be an affectation of his. I watch to see if he does it some more, and I resist the urge to practise it myself to see what it feels like — that could be bordering on psychopathy.

I can't help but feel like I'm being played as a twerp, but I sit through the rest of the meeting in silence. I make a few notes. I'd like to really understand what they are working on, but when I do interject from time to time I get a comment that really means, *Fuck off, this is for us to run and you to watch.*

At the end, after many more cycles of comment, search, discuss, search, silence, Jinny leads a shout of "Sweet Fucking Awesome" to which they all respond "Go For It" and everybody disperses around the various sofas and breakout rooms scattered through the building.

I get back to my desk and I wait for them to drift back. They don't appear. I resign myself to watching the Lazy IM feed as it trickles through.

Vasi complains about the weather and posts a short repeating video of some kid shaking his fist at the rain.

Carl responds with a clip of a toddler pole dancing, falling flat on his face, then taking a bow. He asks if anybody is considering coming to see his end-of-month routine, and receives immediate jazz hands responses.

This chain of joke video, question, response, video continues all afternoon and while I watch I look through Sweet's website and technical documentation. The documentation weirdly follows the same anarchic structure of the chat and the meeting. Small nuggets of gold among mountains of crap. I wonder how anybody does anything productive when it's all so directionless, devoid of strategy and control, and seems to thrive on interruption by Lazy.

I'm taken with the Lazy website. It's tagline is "Productivity Enhancement For Productive Teams." I wonder if it's deliberately ironic.

Before I leave for home, I get my very own IM from Amber. It's my first. I am unexcited by it. But I am resigned that this will be one of many, many more. I've seen the way the team works and they would cease to function if you took Lazy away. It would be like taking the stabilisers off a three-year-old's bike and laughing as they set off. Slowly and surely, the bike would tip over and dump the kid into a crying heap. Yes, it would be funny to take Lazy away — something to create a giphy from — but the business would stop functioning. Odd to think it's so reliant on a messaging app when all you have to do is get your arse off the chair and go and talk to someone.

Amber is asking if I'm still in the office and whether we could catch up. I've noticed in my few days here that everything is a 'catchup'. It's like a byword for any kind of meeting you could ever want. I wonder if it's because nobody wants to admit that work is happening anywhere. You can't have a project meeting if you can have a much more friendly 'catchup'. Where did this come from? And there's an implication with 'catchup' that at least one of you isn't aware of what the meeting is about. That you are in fact behind with the facts and need to 'catchup'. Why not just call these things what they are, and if you can't come up with a name that in some way reflects the point of the meeting, it's a good indicator that the meeting is pointless.

But I'm curious what Amber might be wanting to 'catchup' about, so I reply that "I'm free until 5," which is sort of a lie and sort of the truth since I am free until five but I'm free after five as well — but I'd just rather go home.

She says she'll meet me in The Wizard Of Oz and I instantly receive a Lazy invitation to a meeting in The Wizard of Oz, and click on the 'Accept' button. Well, at least she has asked for a meeting. She could have tried to conduct the whole thing in the IM app with giffys, jiffys, emoticons, emojis and TLMs — that's Three Letter Mnemonics to you people not versed in IT speak — so I'm thankful for that. By way of explanation, we had TLMs well before the internet and they are still very popular. Of course they've been superseded somewhat by TLAs (Three Letter Abbreviations/Acronyms) and FLMs (Four Letters) but they still serve the intended purpose of keeping prying eyes away from what you are doing and making sure those that need to know are kept out of the loop; the millennials have made them into an artform.

Anyway, Amber is already sitting in the meeting room typing into the obligatory laptop.

"Hey Jack. How's it going?"

She asks effusively, as if I'm the only person in the world she is interested in right now and what I am about to say is the most important sentence ever to be uttered by a middle-aged man in a T-shirt. But then she carries on tapping into the laptop without me replying. I think I might have had time to nod.

"That's great. Great. I'm glad you're settling in." She pulls a face and looks down at her laptop. "Look. I wanted to talk to you about something that's come up." She pouts. "You see. Somebody's said something that I want to run by you? You know. Um … get your side of the story."

"Crikey," I say.

"Oh! No! It's not like that," she says. She fiddles with a pen, tips her head ever so slightly to one side like when a dog hears a whistle. She smiles. "Not yet, anyway."

So, it is exactly like 'that' then.

"You see," she begins, "we think all our staff are Sweet Fucking Awesome, don't we?"

"Sure." Did I respond quickly enough without rolling my eyes? I hope so. She seems to have noticed the hesitancy, though, because she says, "No. But we really do, don't we?"

I'm feeling a little uncomfortable. I mean, yes, sure everybody is awesome aren't they? In a sort of *let's have some fun with words and have a laugh* kind of way. But nobody takes this crap seriously? I inspect her face. It's sheet white. Not sure if that's the vampire makeup, but she seems to think this sort of thing is vital to the running of the universe and is going to protect it like Cerberus protects the bones of the dead.

"Yes, we do," I say. I try to sound sincere. Like the day they asked me if I wanted the job. I put my voice into deep baritone male and enunciate each word as clearly as I can. I inwardly cringe that I've perhaps overdone it.

"So. When we think everybody is awesome, what do you think it means about trust?"

"Sorry, Amber. I don't know what you're getting at. I think I went through this with Freya during the induction."

"Okay, Jack. I'll spell it out to help you. If everybody is awesome and we all believe that to be true…" she's nodding along as she says this, like one of those plastic dogs on the parcel shelf of a Vauxhall Astra, "…it means we trust them to do their work, without needing to check up on them."

I'm gobsmacked. "Er–"

"Somebody has complained — and I can't say who at this stage, and if this conversation goes well that will be the end of it. Apparently you asked what they were working on and how long it would take them. Now, we see that as a failure of trust."

Oh, for fuck's sake. You have got to be kidding me.

"But I'm a manager," I say.

"Well, it's a squad master, not a manager. The most important thing here is that we follow the company behaviours. Do you agree that asking humans to justify their time is not quite the behaviour we want, given that we trust everybody?"

I don't know what to say. I know what I want to do. And that's to punch her stupid fucking lights out. But I reckon that's inappropriate. This is like some dystopian comedy show. I'm feeling confused and angry. I want to say so.

"Well I don't think I agree with you."

She purses her lips and bows her head, ever so slightly. If she had glasses on she would now be looking over the top of them like my old headmaster used to do when we kicked a ball inside the classroom or threw an ink splat at the whiteboard.

I continue. "I have to know what they are working on to make sure it's actually progressing the company. You can see that, can't you?"

"Look. I've got a couple of suggestions of books for you to read. But what we know is that full autonomy and full trust leads to full performance. It's not enough to just say the behaviours like we've learnt them on a training course. We have to believe them and act on them."

I don't know where she gets these soundbites from. Some sort of online bullshit generator, probably. But I can see she's deadly serious. Her eyes are narrowed like a dog watching a ball, and her lips are stretched so thin they've disappeared. I've been here a week, I've just resolved to do my best (like a cub scout, but let's not go there), and most importantly I've promised myself I wouldn't fuck up — for Em's sake.

So I say, "Well of course. I'd be really happy to read anything you suggest, Amber. Thanks."

I may have laid it on a bit thick, because she tips her head ever so slightly to one side — it's like that dog again, the one that doesn't quite understand what you've told it, but is happy you're talking in its direction — she's weighing me up. I bet she's thinking I'm brontosaurus Jack Cooper.

She says, "I'm watching you, and if you so much as trample the wrong fern, or take a bath in the wrong lake, I'm going to set the T-Rex free and he's gonna tear the flesh from your bones and make you into a leather easy-chair for the young 'uns to have a breakout catchup in."

But she doesn't, of course, actually say any of that. Instead she tells me she's going to send me the links and says, "I think some of these are in the Sweet Library. I'm sure you'll enjoy them."

That night, I sit alone at home. I want to go to the Flying Pig but I resist the temptation and instead watch TV. Em is at the top of my mind, but I'm afraid of calling her.

I send her a text: "So sorry. Mum told me the news. I'm happy for you. Call me. Love you, Dad xx"

Em's told me before that I don't need to sign off every text because she knows it's from me. But it seems incomplete if I don't, and too short to be a proper, worthy message.

I send the text and part of my mind cannot watch TV for watching the phone to see if it suddenly vibrates with an incoming message. Between programmes, I pick it up and make sure I haven't missed a reply, but Em keeps silent. This must be what it's like for all those kids on their devices. Constant anxiety over when the next message will come in. Eventually I fall asleep.

6

When I get up, I check my phone to see if Em has responded to my text. She hasn't. Vodafone has sent me some more offers for *Thoughtful Thursday* or *Funfilled Friday* or something. I delete them. I wonder if it's possible to charge them for taking space on my phone or something.

I read the text I sent Em last night to see if I really sent it or if, through some rift in space time, it has decided to remain unsent. Every indication suggests the text has gone.

I read it again. Fuck. Why did I start with "So Sorry." She could take that to mean I was sorry about the pregnancy, not sorry for my behaviour. Fuckity Fuck.

I quickly send another text. "I mean I'm sorry about the argons and how I rated, I'm not sorry about you being present." I press send.

Fucking spell check. Fuck.

I'm panicking. "Spell chequers". Delete. "Spell Checkers. Ha Ha. I mean, I'm sorry about the argument and how I reacted. I'm happy about you being pregnant." I double check and triple check. Then press send.

I watch the phone while I eat breakfast, but by eight o'clock there's no reply. I huff about a bit, not quite knowing what to do next, and then I decide to send a gift. Something that's not open to interpretation; something straightforward, simple, that simply says, "I love you and I'm thinking of you and I'm sorry," without actually saying it.

A cuddly bear!

Fuck no! Buying gifts for Em is fraught with consumer and climate morality traps. But surely she can't complain about a gift for the baby. After some searching online I settle on a crinkly book with "textures, sound and visual delights for your cherished one," and I send it to her with a suitable card.

Then I set off for Sweet, and when I arrive I have a catchup with Baked-Beans Freya scheduled. I know because it's in my calendar and I have received a Lazy message saying she's waiting for me in Casablanca. I check the time, and I'm only a couple of minutes late so, mindful of the meeting the day before, I take my laptop and circle the building looking for a room called Casablanca. It's tucked behind the lower-floor kitchen next to the coats and can only sit four people around a small circular table covered in vivid green formica.

It's just me and Freya.

She looks up from her laptop as I enter.

"Hey, Jack. Be with you in a sec."

I sit down and watch her. She's every bit as attractive today as before. She's wearing a Sweet-green T-shirt with *Cast Champion* emblazoned in some kind of horror-font across her chest. The company slogan "Sweet FA" is just above her left nipple which, I'm slightly ashamed to notice, is pushing at the T-shirt fabric ever so slightly. Well, I notice these things. I'm a heterosexual male. I think about the baked beans again, put my laptop on the table and open it up. As the lid hinges upward, I feel like I'm just beginning to fit in. If I could send a Lazy message while holding a meeting and answer a text all at once, I'd be right in with the in-crowd.

We go through all the standard openings about how we both are, how I'm finding the team, is there anything I need. You know. Same stuff as always and I'm trying to answer, not look at her nipple, keep smiling and say some coherent things. But I find that by avoiding looking down at her chest and concentrating on what she says, I'm staring at her lips. And what lips. Not too plump, like some of those ridiculous labia stick-ons that were fashionable a few years back, but not thin and mean either. Just right. Girl-next-door kind of look.

She's wearing toned lipstick. A couple of years ago I heard the word *nude* used to describe lipstick, maybe because it's not really a colour change, just a shininess. Satin, I'd say. And her satin lips contrast with the white of her teeth, which I watch as they gently move up and down in time with her words. It's safe to say I find her very attractive. I wonder what it would be like to kiss her. There and then. Just reach over the table and kiss her lips. It doesn't really bear thinking about in this PC, post-millennial, alt-corporate, hashtag-dominated world, but I take comfort that the thoughts are my own. She cannot read them, or see them, and I know from years of experience she has no idea what I'm thinking about.

"Why are you staring at my mouth, Jack? Will you stop it? It's making me very uncomfortable."

To say I am mortified would be an understatement of all understatements. Using a word such as mortified is like calling WWII a hiccup in international relations, or describing Hurricane Sandy as a breeze. I am destroyed, humiliated, embarrassed, fucked and buggered all at once. The blood leaves my feet and rushes up my back like a red Formula One car going into the long straight at Brands Hatch. As it races up my spine, the hairs on my hairs stand on end. By the time I fully comprehend the situation, Freya's words and my limbic system's response to the threat, I have a ruby-red face, scarlet ears and a mouth so wide open it could accommodate the 3:45 Paddington to Truro HST.

"Err. Um. Oh," I stammer. Or at least I think I do. I don't know what I actually say, and I can't analyse the situation quickly enough to establish if I should apologise, challenge, burst into tears, rush out of the room or — wild outrageous idea — admit what's going on.

And as the thought of admission crosses my mind, it pops into those neurons that occasionally act on their own without remorse, embarrassment, control, impedance or inhibitions, and lands in a place where the devil sits; a place where abandon is king and self-destruction is queen.

I say, "I'm sorry, but I find you incredibly sexy. Your lips are really kissable."

Inappropriate actions have dogged my life. The part of my brain responsible for inhibiting what comes out of my mouth, or preventing me doing some stupid thing, sometimes dramatically misfires. It's not all the time, and it's not often, but it seems to be at moments of high personal cost where my brain, unbeknown to me, takes the stress out of the situation by exploding it once and for all. No longer able to deal with the long-term and low-key anxiety some situations bring, this part of my brain very much prefers to set light to the fuse and take the consequences.

This is not to say it's self-destruction for the sake of blowing things up. There is analysis behind it. Analysis in the form of justification. I might say to myself; this person really doesn't get it, I think I owe it to them and all their peers and superiors to point out how fucking stupid they are. Or when answering a question about a product in a hall of potential customers, I might just tell the truth with something like, I don't use this product myself, I prefer competitor X because it lets me do such and such. It's true. I don't use the product. And of course there are a large number of salespeople out there that don't use their company's products because they find something else superior. But in the normal course of daily business, you're simply not allowed to say such things out loud.

But I sometimes do. I sometimes think it might be a form of autism, or social inability — on the spectrum, a mild syndrome — you know, like all the things we say about little Johnny to excuse his continuous fucking awful behaviour when he pours nail polish on the bathroom floor, or throws apple cores under the sofa to rot, or strangles a friend's pet half to death. It's a blindness to social politics linked to an inability to lie, just to smooth things over and keep the peace. It's schadenfreude for when you tell the absolute truth about something that nobody expects, and watch the fallout. But the fallout often engulfs the messenger.

This behaviour has become more frequent in recent years. When I sit in contemplation, I realise it's probably responsible for a lot of my problems, and I think it's become more prevalent because (a) I'm older and see things a little more clearly through a lens of experience, (b) some of my neurons have probably degenerated, killed by alcohol, environmental toxins, pesticides, lead from cars and micro particles from the back end of clean-certified diesel engines, and this means my inhibitor circuits have been replaced by holes, (c) I'm angry about everything that *silence* stands for.

I'm angry that Volkswagen gamed the pollution tests on cars, I'm angry that the IPCC frames its advice in realpolitik while the planet heats, I'm angry that the EU won't act decisively on emissions because of global trade deals, I'm furious that plastic is bunging up the rivers and oceans. But most of all I'm angry that so-called intelligent people don't even raise these issues. Good people don't stand up tall and call it out, in fact, good people deliberately obfuscate and deny. And that makes me angry. It's a deep anger that only sometimes surfaces, but I think that the inhibitory part of my brain has a hotline to it.

The internet was supposed to fix many of these things. In the great birth of free access to information, it was thought it would become impossible to hide things. That corporations would be unable to keep their subterfuge secret, that governments would be unable to cover up poverty statistics, and that action on all these issues would follow as the blanket of secrecy was withdrawn and replaced with the polythene sheet of transparency. But it was not the case. The internet quickly became a place where all the world's cranks, deniers, perverts, criminals, dictators, forgers, dealers, stamp collectors and trainspotters could find each other and exchange information. Before the internet it was abnormal to be abnormal, but all of a sudden nutters could find each other, create a community and discuss ways to perfect their trade. Abnormality was normalised.

And I had a part in this normalisation of perversion. I. Me. Mea culpa. And so did everybody working in the IT industry and computer sciences. Yes, we were enabling good, but we enabled evil too. It turns out the internet is not neutral. As fakery, forgery and perversion blossomed online, so the good stuff withered on a forgotten vine.

Now, this tirade is not intended to get you calling up the BBC and the *Guardian* — though that would be nice — it's intended to show how angry I have become. The anger runs through me like shit through a sewage pipe, and it rears its head at ridiculous times by helping me to duck out of difficult situations. Like this one. You may think I've just been strangely inappropriate in an office situation, but really my brain is trying to get me out of the commitment I made to my daughter. It's sabotaging my behaviour so I can look my daughter in the eye and say it wasn't my fault, they took my comments the wrong way and now I've been sacked. Because, inside, I know that a comment like this is probably a sackable offence, or at least one that will gather me a written warning. Businesses take sexual harassment seriously these days. You can argue about whether it was sexual harassment or not, but that would be to miss the point. I have deliberately overstepped the line to (a) try and get sacked, and (b) have an excuse for breaking my vow to Em. I suppose also, the fact that Freya is attractive means there is (c) an off chance I might get to have dinner with a sexy woman because all my other options have been closed off and Freya is in front of me.

So now that's all out in the open, what does Freya actually do? I think she has a few options. She can slap me round the face, but that seems like unreconstructed 1970s Benny Hill-inspired behaviour and I'm guessing she's moved on from that sort of thing.

Perhaps she will ignore the comment and carry on; her point has been made, I've been brutally honest about my motivations and you can't fault honesty.

Then maybe she will leave the room without saying anything. Is it now possible for her to continue the conversation? Given I don't yet know what the meeting is about, I guess that's a debatable point. If, unknown to me, she had called this meeting to discuss the unstated sexual chemistry between us that she'd seen from the moment we first met, and wanted to get it out in the open before it affected our working relationship, then my comment might well be seen as an opening gambit in a short, blistering and filthy encounter between consenting adults. On the other hand, if this was a conversation about Sweet and the work I was employed to do — which I seriously think it was — then it is entirely possible I will have made her so uncomfortable that she'll run from the room without another word being said.

I look at her.

It's her turn to go red. She looks over to the door to avoid my gaze. I think she might be going for the leave-the-room option, the complaint to management and the warning or even sacking. I start to feel sick. The inhibition centre of my brain is starting to work again and I am suddenly distressed by my behaviour.

"Ah, ah ah …" I stammer. Stammering is clearly my thing today. What a twat.

And then Freya stands up.

"Jack. Omigod. That is sooo unacceptable. We don't allow sexist talk here. What do you think is going to happen now?" She states this quietly. Almost meanly. "Unbelievable." She shakes her head and begins collecting the pens, paper, and her phone.

She quietly closes the lid of her laptop, picks up her things and walks out of the door with her arms and possessions folded over her chest.

She makes a parting comment, "I think you'd better go home."

Well. At least I know the option she took. One I hadn't considered. An icy professionalism.

I am deeply ashamed.

Isolated.

I sit in the room for five minutes. I am still. Quiet. Contemplative. And slowly the shaming nature of my situation crescendos. I close my eyes and try to focus on what to do next, but all I can think about is Em and Caroline. Em because I have recklessly put my commitment to her in danger, even though she is as yet unaware that I have made the commitment. And Caroline because … well, because after all we've been through she is still what the films and novels call a soul-mate. She is there within me; she always has been, since we met, and I know she always will be. My behaviour, her behaviour, my thoughts and demons, none of it can undo our shared journey through this perilous and often painful thing we call existence.

What a time to be nostalgic for a former partner.

I put my face in my hands and I can feel the tears beneath the surface, just behind my eyes, like a pressure.

But I don't cry.

I close my laptop, leave the room, walk slowly to my desk with my arms and laptop wrapped around my chest, pick up my coat, and leave the building without looking at anybody.

I've utterly fucked it.

7

When you go through a life-changing moment — a crisis, or a moment of intense happiness, like when your child is born, or you hear your wife is having an affair, or perhaps you tell a work colleague you fancy them and she storms out of the room to Lazy-IM everybody about what an arse you are — it's curious to see the rest of the world carrying on as if nothing of importance has happened.

You would think that the world would stop, offer support, congratulations, encouragement or perhaps anger. You hope that the people you pass are intimately aware of the happenings and are affected, not as intensely perhaps, but in a way that shows we are all in this together.

But no, that's not how it goes. As I walk home from Sweet, the most notable interaction I get is a V-sign and beep from the driver of a black Mercedes. I get no 'hellos' or 'how are yous'. I get no 'nice day todays' or other friendly, casual greetings. I interact with nobody except another angry fucker in a tin-on-wheels.

I get home, put my keys and wallet on the dining table, make a cup of tea, and put the morning news on the radio; it is devoid of any mention of my intolerable sexist behaviour. And as the day progresses, I forget the nerve-smashing horror of it all and the shock fades slightly — enough, anyway, to allow me to pass the morning in a relatively pain-free state.

At some point, I think about Em and her ultimatum. I had imagined that the next conversation would go something like this:

I would joyfully admit a career-catharsis and a newfound commitment to Sweet. I'd say how I'd been enjoying it and how lovely the people were. I would explain how I thought the experience, and Sweet's youthful millennialism, would form a great synthesis of achievement, value and personal progress. I would explain how, though tricky at first, I had navigated the wide digital waters separating generations, built a bridge and was busy running trucks back and forward in a giant trade of inter-generational insights for the good of the company.

She would express her delight that I had taken her advice and committed to the new job. She'd say how I was looking younger and spritely, and that it must be good for me. She'd probably hint that Caroline would find the change refreshing and might also find me more attractive. I would laugh at the comment and ignore it, as usual.

She'd ask about the company and the people I work with, and I'd explain all the quirky things they did. We'd talk about the company logos and statements, and how I first thought they were ridiculous but on reflection have decided they serve a useful purpose in creating a shared vision and communicating a set of behaviours among the humans that work there.

Together we would make a lovely dinner. She would chop red peppers and onions, and I would whisk up a delicious vegetarian stir fry that was tasty and satisfying. We'd eat, chat and laugh, and then we'd sit all evening watching an Instagram feed about cats sitting on vacuum cleaners and dogs jumping on beds when their owners had gone out for the day.

Well. That's what I imagined was going to happen. But that was before I fucked the whole thing up and opened my rail-car-sized gob.

Fuck.

I check my phone to see if Em has replied to any of my previous messages and she hasn't. But I do have a text from an unknown number. Vodafone? Not this time. And it's nobody selling stuff either. It's Freya.

And just as I'm about to read it, the door opens and Em steps through.

She's carrying the crinkly book I sent her, but she's not smiling.

She sits down on the same chair she knocked over last time she left the flat. "Dad, what were you thinking by sending a present?"

I don't know what she's on about. She sounds slightly angry but pleased too. I don't know which emotion to respond to or if I'm completely wrong about both of them. Maybe there is a female emotion that combines both anger and pleasure all at once but which I wasn't previously aware of — and then I chastise myself for thinking sexist thoughts.

I shrug. "Err …"

"It's bad luck to buy a baby present until it's born. You should know that."

Yes. I suppose I did know that.

She puts the crinkly book on the shelf by the kitchen window. "You can keep it here for now," she says.

But it wasn't really about the baby, it was about me and her. I'm thinking about how to put the sentiment into words when she says, "I suppose it was really to say sorry to me," and as ever, I'm thankful for her insight.

I nod.

"That's really sweet, Dad. I suppose Mum told you?"

I nod.

She looks at me quizzically then rattles off a bunch of questions that I don't have time to respond to: "Are you okay? Job going all right? Why are you at home? I was going to just drop the present off with a rude note but … do you want to talk? What's happened? Is there something I can do to help? Is it Mum?"

"Wow! That's some list of questions."

She laughs.

"Which one shall I answer first?"

Now it's her turn to shrug. I guess gestures run in families, just like looks and attitudes.

We have a conversation about work and about how hard it is to fit in with the — air quotes — culture, and how the team don't seem to be doing much and how I'm struggling with the whole deal, but that I'm going to see it through because I want to be a good grandad to the new baby.

"Do you, Dad? Really?"

I see in her doubt how I've failed to give her the security she needs. How I've been a shit, self-obsessed father. In her one comment, I see how she is walking through life frightened and alone and that she deserves a supporting father, not a v-sign and a car horn.

"Of course," I say, and it feels utterly unconvincing so I lean across the table and take her hands. "I'm so excited about the baby. I'm bloody angry about being a grandfather so young, but I can't wait to bounce the little chap on my knee."

"A boy, is it?" She smiles and laughs. "That's presumptuous. And you're not as young as you think, old man."

"I don't care if it's a xenomorph with a Wolverine hairdo, I'm going to love the last furry hair on its body with all my heart."

"You think it might be furry, do you? And you'll still love it?"

I stare at her. She's got that mischievous Em-face that means I've fallen into her trap. A kinked smile beneath bright eyes. Actually, it reminds me of her mother.

I realise that whatever I say next is vitally important. I know she's spun a web for me, but I can't avoid flying right in. It's too late to manoeuvre.

"I might have to buy a ten-pack of Gillette disposables to cope. But I promise, I'm going to be the best grandad this side of Trump's wall."

She seems happier — there's nothing like mixing a bit of politics into an emotional discussion to make Em happy — and she leans over to give me a peck on the cheek. She smiles and pats her belly.

"Only six months."

This talk of being a good grandparent — and by extension a better father — makes us both smile. I love it. It makes me feel good, and I get a rush of enthusiasm for my new job and the people at Sweet. It's like the fog of cynicism has been blown away. Jobs are not real life. But family is.

And then I remember why I'm at home.

"What is it, Dad?"

I can't keep anything from Em. The slightest waver in my eyes is enough for her to catch on to something. I'd carefully skirted round the details of my short day at work and now I don't know quite how to tell her. I'm embarrassed.

"Oh, just suddenly remembered I have a meeting. I've got to do some preparation."

"PowerPoint?"

I laugh. "Nothing so ancient."

We have a quick cuppa and then she leaves. This time without bashing furniture. She's happy that I'm supporting her, but I'm in despair about repairing the damage I've done.

I remember the text still waiting unread on my phone.

"Jack. We need to talk and put our relationship on a professional footing once more. A reset. Everybody makes mistakes, and that's okay, as long as we learn from them. I think it would be best if this conversation happened informally away from the office. Can you meet me at Foxglove at 6 p.m. this evening, after work? It has some quiet areas to talk. I've not yet made a complaint, so let's see how the conversation goes? Let me know if this is okay."

Shit.

Now what.

Part of me is relieved. There is still hope.

But the part of my brain responsible for sabotaging the gig is now furious and angry. It's saying, Hey, WTF, (it uses millennial speak of course), I thought I'd fucked this up for you so you didn't have to suffer the indignity of working in a shit place with shit people who all think they are your superiors and think you're a worthless old twat with no relevance in today's internet-driven society and workplace. Now you're facing years of humiliation working under young bosses with less knowledge who don't listen to a word you say and don't give you credit when things you do turn out to be right. That place is a haven for wasting-snowflakes who think a hard day's work is a reference to a Beatles album in their grandparents' LP collection — if they give it any thought at all. Is that something you really want to go back to when I've engineered a perfectly good way out? And for heaven's sake, don't worry about Em. She'll be fine. She'll be back in a few days trying to manipulate a meeting between you and Caroline. But if you go back to that place you're finished.

I didn't appreciate the lecture. Not from my own head. It bored me. I've heard it all before and I'm a bit sick of it. Yes, that part of my brain knows how to pull my levers and keep me from acting in my own best interests, but I'm over it.

I really am over it. Em was right when she said I'm killing myself. If I don't shape up, I'll die early and that arsehole in the Mercedes at the zebra crossing will probably honk his horn at my funeral car going slow across a junction. Why should I be alone? And so what if I have a younger boss and my team think I'm a moron. I *am* a moron. Get over it.

I was liking my defence here. Feeling powerful, strong, in touch and invincible.

I start a reply to the text.

"Hi Freya, thanks for your text." No, that's shit. Umm …

"Thanks Freya, you're right we need to talk, I was such a t …" No.

Um. Commas? In a text? That's so old-fucker.

"Cheers. You really did look fab, you …" Fucking stop it.

"I'm so sorry …" Weak!

What is it that I want to say, exactly? That I'm sorry. No. That she's right. No. I just want to accept her peace offering. I look up Foxglove and it's a mile down the road, near Forest Park.

"Freya. Jack here. Yes. Thats a good idea. Ill see you then." It's short, it's to the point without being weak, without being pompous and without commas or apostrophes … oh, hang on. Is that bit about it being a good idea, a good idea? I take it out.

"Freya. Jack here. Yes, I'll see you then." This is too short and looks wrong. Man, this is hard, when did accepting an invitation become so fucking difficult?

"I accept." No. Even shorter, and she might find it combative or rude.

"I can make that, Freya. I'll see you at 6. Cheers Jack." Cheers, is that right word to sign off with? Not, Thanks? Or just, Jack. I try it.

"I can make that, Freya. See you at 6. Jack." Not as friendly, but I think better. I can leave any further apology or explanation to later.

I press send, and I watch the phone for a minute hoping I've done the right thing, and that there isn't some secret texting protocol I've broken that causes offense. Well if there is …

The phone vibrates.

A text from Freya.

:-)

I think that's good.

I am super nervous from about four o'clock onwards and I start going through my wardrobe looking for something to wear. It has to be smart, but not too smart, it can't look like I'm going out for the evening, that would be a disastrous choice. No, it has to look like I've come from work; as if I'd been at work all day instead of worrying myself to death at home.

I choose a pair of jeans, but when I put them on I think they are probably too old fashioned. I've noticed the millennial men wearing super tight jeans cropped halfway up their calf with jazzy socks showing above plimsoles — Jesus, does anybody even know what a plimsole is anymore? These jeans are Levi 501s boot style. Basically, that means they are comfortable around the middle and don't make my legs feel like they have stockings on. And let's face it, my old man has a bit of freedom to wobble. It needs a bit of room down there.

But when I look at these jeans from the perspective of trying to make a serious impression on somebody who holds my future in her hands, they scream out old-fucker. I try on the beige chinos that I usually reserve for going out in the evenings. No. Too dressy. It's not a date. What about that pair of green cargoes I've never worn before. I try them on, but then have nothing I could possibly put on as a shirt. Nothing matches.

I settle on the jeans. They are the least-worst option and at least a lot of the people at Sweet wear jeans (particularly the older ones) even if the cut is not as modern as it could be. I can go with retro.

Next problem is the top. Shirt or T-shirt? I try on a succession of T-shirts starting with the *Space Invaders* Sweet-green top that I wore on day two. It doesn't smell fresh so it's reassigned to the washing basket, and the others are variations on themes of untidy, unkempt, unironed, unwashed un … just … fucking unimpressive.

So I try some shirts. I figure that as long as I don't tuck the shirt in at the belt, I can get away with it. It's not young man's territory perhaps, but there is some style and gravitas to a shirt that I think will help. I choose a shirt that's more casual than dressy, with a soft collar which I wear open at the neck.

I check myself in the mirror. That'll do pig.

I get undressed again, place my clothes on the bed and spend the next two hours wasting time among short bursts of getting ready. Shower, shave, coffee, TV. You know. I've time to waste, but I don't want to be hurried along at the last minute in a panic and end up being late.

In the end, I arrive at Foxglove fifteen minutes early and find Freya already sitting in a booth with a glass of red nearly finished in front of her, and she's texting on her phone. She's wearing a white blouse over blue jeans. Her hair falls deliciously onto her shoulders and she puts down her phone and flashes me a smile as she sees me walking towards her.

"Hi."

"Hi." I smile. Sort of smile, sort of grimace disguised as a smile. I forcibly stop myself from checking out her lips, chest or face. I look her right in the eyes, and when, after a moment, that becomes uncomfortable, I look around the bar and say, "Nice place."

"Yes."

I didn't expect the wine. I think maybe I shouldn't drink anything, but then how would that be perceived. Anti-social? Sensible? Grown up? Fuck, I don't know. I'm going to go for it. I could do with a glass. "Um. Can I get you another?" I say and point at the glass. "What was it?"

"Just a cab sav, thanks."

Thank fuck. The pressure is off for the moment. I retreat to the bar and get two glasses of cab sav. The bar is almost empty and I'm back again in just a couple of minutes. I sit down opposite.

We start talking simultaneously …

"Let me just say—"

"I wanted to—"

Then we both stop at the same time.

We laugh.

"You go," I say.

She takes a sip of wine. "I'm sorry I overreacted. You

were just being honest."

What? Really? She's apologising. I pick up my glass and take sip, trying to keep my face from revealing the relief, but also the horror. She really ought not to be the one to apologise. I put the glass down with a tap on the table.

I say, "No. No. It's not you who should apologise. I was wrong to say what I said. It was unprofessional and–" I stop. I try to think of the right words to say next. What I desperately want to say is that I have this streak of self-destruction a mile wide, running up and down my spine and into my brain, and that I was just voicing my fear of failure after years of being trapped in a toilet-bound career. I want to say how it was an attempt at getting rid of the pressure of having to be a grown up for my daughter and her new baby, and I want to explain how my marriage has collapsed, my son is a lunatic, I'm a failure, and I'm now desperately scared of giving anything a proper go.

"Sorry." I think all of those thought processes were in that word somewhere. "It was inappropriate and it won't happen again."

Freya smiles and takes another drink. "Well, that's okay then," she says cheerfully. "We'd better get to know each other so we can behave professionally in future."

Is she flirting? Subtly? Did her eyes twinkle? Just slightly? When she said "professionally", was there an ironic stress, or an unspoken set of air quotes? I dare to look at her lips for an extra clue. She has lippy on and a detectable brush of blusher on her cheeks. Her blouse is open at the neck and gapes ever so slightly to reveal the hint of breast. Fuck. Baked fucking beans. This is surely not happening.

"Um. Yes, yes." I repeat myself like a demented parrot. "Okay. Um. How long have you been at Sweet?" It's the best I can do in the circumstances — a desperate attempt to give the conversation to her, so I can spend some time in my own head instead of attempting to make conversation. It occurs to me — and you may say "finally, you moron" — that Freya has engineered the entire meeting not for apologies, or because she wants to talk about the incident, but because she wanted a date. No sooner has that thought crossed my mind than I dismiss it. Even if true, I couldn't afford to act on the information. If there was the tiniest, most miniscule chance I was wrong, it would be game over, man.

So I sit back with my wine, and I listen. I avoid watching her lips or her open-at-the-neck blouse and I nod and smile and look her in the eye. Into the blue spectacular eyes of a hot crush. A crush that I cannot let on I have. Not again, and not yet, at least.

"It's two years, now," she says. She moves her hair behind her ear as she says this and looks upwards at nothing in particular. "I love it. I love all the humans there and the fantastic culture we've created. All the other Cast Champions are awesome."

Yes, she calls them humans! It's like some sort of anti-sexist, anti-sex, multi-cultural inclusiveness. A bland, judgement-devoid, quality-removed, plain, ordinary word just in case any other noun chosen might possibly, even ever so slightly, result in offence to somebody, somewhere. I let it pass. And anyway, I'm busy avoiding the lure of her open-neck top and full lips.

She explains that a happy cast makes a productive, profitable company based on autonomy, mastery and purpose, and that to get profits you only need to focus on the happiness of the humans that work for you.

"Don't you just love that we work in a place where they value the well-being of the staff over directly controlling what they do?"

I nod. I'm not really listening.

She says, "Success vindicates that love conquers all."

Okay. So at this point I'm not quite sure what she really says, but I'm sure it has "vindicates" in it. If it had been anybody other than a sexy brunette, a decade or two younger than me with kissable lips, I would have been calling bullshit by the second sip of wine. But instead I find myself purring over the words that slip from her lips like honey from … no scratch that, honey's the wrong metaphor for words slipping from lips. I don't want to compound the bullshit with a pile of my own. But I do want to explain how I am caught up in the warm positivity and enthusiasm of it all, and not just because she reminds me of a plate of baked beans.

And then it's my turn to talk about me. I start slowly, have a break while she goes to the bar for a round — and comes back with a bottle which we use to fill up our glasses to the brim — then bang on in very general terms about my previous jobs, how I came to get into team management and finally ended up at Sweet. I don't say that I've really no idea how I got the job because I seem to fit in like a climate change CNN reporter at a Trump rally.

In a convenient pause where I'm talking about the first time I worked in a company selling software on the internet, and have run out of words from sheer boredom at my own dullness, she says, "We all thought your online profile was amazing. Done so well. So beautiful. But–"

She stops herself like she's about to say something I shouldn't hear.

I can't imagine where she's going with this. I've seen my CV. Not surprising, since I put it together. It's okay, I guess, but I wouldn't give me a job at Sweet even if I was advertising for me.

"Yes?" I say.

"You know. It's like, well … when we had that meeting this morning, I thought maybe we'd all got it wrong. That you weren't who we thought you were."

"I'm just me. Bad judgement sometimes, it's true." I take a big glug of wine. It's going down really well. I like this place and I like her company. She's easy to be with, and funny. And she's fearsome in her love for all things Sweet. With the wine flowing and gently mocking my senses, we begin talking about personal stuff — boyfriends, wives, daughters. She's had a series of boyfriends who were all arseholes — every single one of them, it seems. She's never been married, is thirty-five, lives on her own just out of town in a small cottage with a pond and a cat.

I tell her about my separation, Caroline, Em's determination to get us back together (we both laugh a bit nervously at this), the extension on the family home, my flat with a shower that has so little pressure it's like washing your hair with a water pistol.

And then at some point she asks, "You have a son as well, don't you?"

"I don't talk about him."

"Oh. Why not?"

"I just don't. Can we drop the topic?"

I say this line a bit aggressively to close her off, and she picks up her glass and sips. A distinctly icy atmosphere descends, and within five minutes she's looking at her watch and saying it's time to call it a night. She leaves with half a bottle of wine still on the table.

I finish it off, and top it up with some whisky chasers. I think somewhere in that evening I raise a toast to baked beans. But maybe not.

Now I bet you're wondering why I haven't really talked about my son before and why I won't talk to Freya about him.

It's because he's a furry.

I've disowned him. I cannot explain just how ashamed I am.

He is smart. Smarter than I'll ever be. He was on track to get a double first at Warwick in economics and philosophy when he just left. Somewhere along the way he discovered some internet sub-culture and got the idea in his head that he could make a lovely life for himself by becoming a bear — an otherkin, apparently.

I am so angry. Still. All that potential, all that study, schooling, thought, analysis, and he now makes a pathetic living sewing teddy bear costumes for people to dress up at weekend fetish conferences. It's a travesty. Being gender neutral is one thing. Living your life in a fur suit is another.

His otherkin name is Geronimo the Bear. I wish I was joking. I wish this was a bad dream and that one day I'll wake up, but it's not and I won't.

Oscar turns up one day with a cartoon furry bear head, paws for gloves, and a stubby tail pinned to the back of his jeans. The oversized eyes on the head remind me of that rolling eyes emoji. It's got round, brown ears and a white streak asymmetrically arranged down one side of the face. He puts the head on and parades around the kitchen striking bear poses.

"Growl."

"You're a bit old for this, Oscar." I look up from the pasta dinner or whatever it is.

"You got your best moany-old-man hat on today then, Dad?"

I'm used to this sort of comment, and I let it go.

"Put the paws on. I think all of us are non-human in part," he says.

I come back to this part of the memory over and over. Should I have taken an interest? Complimented the bear on its anthropomorphic quality, perhaps. Maybe tried the gloves on and conducted a few bear-inspired swipes or dance moves. Fuck, I don't know. What should I have done?

All I know is what I did say: "Can you get these fucking things off the table and sit down and eat your dinner like a bloody adult." I pick up one of the paws and throw it towards the kitchen bin.

After that, he started showing up regularly in full fur. He wanted to be called Geronimo, his new 'fursona', and he called me old-fleshie. It would have been funny if he'd been four, but he was a grown twenty-one-year-old. It just snowballed until he was more in the suit than out, gave up uni and started selling fur costumes on the internet.

He made it his life.

And I felt it was just to taunt me.

I ask the question of myself. The question I have avoided facing up to by making sure any discussion with Caroline or Em ended in an argument before it was brought up. The question: Was it all my attitude? I wonder if that single moment caused more damage and arguments than a thousand Brexit referendums. Should I have simply accepted my son's wishes and moved on? And would that have saved all the aggravation? Would that have confined Geronimo to a few furred-up weekends in a town hall, and would that have stopped the prostitution, the affair, the separation, the drinking, the depression, and the estrangement between me and my son? Who knows?

Caroline managed to move on. In spite of the hurt and

the pain, as if somebody had stolen our wonderful son and put a fucking teddy bear in his place, Oscar/Geronimo lives in the family home and Caroline seems happy with the arrangement.

I have never been able to accept it. I cannot look him in the eye. I cannot cope with being in the same room. I cannot talk to him, text or email him. The pain is too fresh, too … painful. It hurts. It still hurts and it's now five years since the trouble started.

Things became increasingly difficult at home. Like all couples bringing up teenagers, we had the usual problems with the Kevin & Perry-type attitude. You know the sort of thing, we've all been there, either when growing up or because we have kids of our own — insolence, ingratitude, not wanting to do anything with the family, mumbling, moaning, sighing, staying out too late, not being in for dinner — this is all a normal expression of independence. I'd still do some of that now if I was living with anybody.

And then there's all the stuff that we as parents of children born near the millennium have to deal with. The preferring to stay on devices rather than talk to anybody, taking mobile phones to bed, looking for wireless connections whenever you go out and wherever you go. It particularly irked me when we had relatives around. Relatives that had sent endless gifts, birthday cards and good wishes, were greeted with shrugs and limp handshakes before the kids dashed back to their phones. I worried that my children's social skills and manners were non-existent. They seemed to be afraid even to call their own friends or go out to meet them.

But the more we tried to intervene, to correct, to sort it out, the worse it seemed to get. And we were never free of it. The internet does not turn off. Mobile phone signals do not turn off. I regret ever having brought some of these things into the house. But we didn't know. Me and Caroline, that is. And I didn't know. I thought it was good for us to be on the cutting edge of technology, because I had been there all my career.

And with the endless, tireless connection to the world, came the fads. The vegetarianism, the veganism, the memes, the vines, the videos, the Snapchats, the blogs the … I can go on and on. The kids got into them all. They were going to be famous influencers and the internet was the route to untold riches.

Oscar — and I won't keep using his furry name if you don't mind — was also into gaming. Games which sucked the life right out of him. He wasn't happy when he wasn't playing, and when he was playing he would rage if he died too early or missed a jump or whatever thing it was he had going on. I lost track.

So I gave up, except in extreme situations when I would attack first and ask questions later. The kids were afraid of me, Caroline was afraid of me, and I was afraid of me. I became increasingly bitter that I had spent half my life rearing children that seemed to want no part in what I had to offer. No part in the way my life had been run, no part in heritage, in history, in family, in fucking anything. Everything they wanted to be part of was dished up by mega-tech firms, funded by advertising, where they spent billions making sure they hooked the young kids in. A drug? A fucking hell on Earth.

And the worst part of it all, was that I understood intimately how this stuff worked, because I had been there at the beginning. I had helped research addictive nudges in computer applications, built programs that kept the user interested with random jingles and rewards. I understood.

And it was abhorrent to everything the silicon revolution was supposed to bring. No social conscience, only the monetisation of society, relationships, family and friends. And perhaps most damaging, it was the monetisation of anxiety and fear by asking that most fundamental of human questions over and over: Do you really belong?

I fucking hate it all.

8

I wake up with a headache, and just for laughs the sun is beating through a gap in the curtains and hitting my eyes like it's Rocky smacking some Russian boxing champ who's trapped on the ropes in the final round. I turn over, groan and take a look at the clock. Eight a.m. Well at least I didn't sleep through the morning. I suppose that's a bonus, depending on how you look at it.

It occurs to me that it's fucking Friyay. Great. I wonder what delights I can expect at Sweet today. However, even though I'm groaning and moaning inside my head about the effects of alcohol after being left sitting on your own in a bar by a beautiful woman, for some inexplicable reason I'm optimistic. Even the sun's Rocky impression isn't enough to stop me from rising, stuffing my mouth with a handful of ibuprofens and paracetamols and humming while I make coffee. I've not hummed for a while; something is going on.

I search through my memories of the night before and rapidly establish the reason for my cheerfulness. Freya. I know it didn't exactly end well, and I could tell she was a bit frosty at me for avoiding the questions about my son, but in other respects we clicked. I like her. She's sexy. I work with her, and the prospect of seeing her again today makes my stomach turn over — in a good way. That's a revived experience I haven't felt for a while.

And when I make it into work, there's another surprise awaiting me. My entire team is assembled; they're sitting at their desks working furiously on their laptops.

"Good morning, frozen mammals!" I say with an enthusiasm they haven't previously seen and which, frankly, surprises me too.

"Hey." One of them says this. I don't know who. Nobody looks up.

"Come on, guys," I persist. "Good morning. How are you?"

I get some recognition. Blood from a stone springs to mind, but it's more like sense from a Trump.

"What's going on, Vasi?" I ask. "Everybody's early and at their desks. Have we got a deadline or something?" Vasi is wearing a dress today. A frock, really. In October? They's full beard is neatly trimmed and lip gloss is shining through a mouth-sized gap in the facial hair. I ignore it. I wait for them to respond.

They looks at me and says, "It's Big Delivery Day."

I'm puzzled.

"You know? BDD?"

"No."

"We get the day to work on our own projects. Anything we like."

"Anything?"

"Sure. Who knows where good ideas come from?"

"Is this like an innovation thing?"

"I guess. The cast works on anything they want. Most of the guys tend to pick projects that relate to their work, but not everybody. There's a kick off in twenty minutes in the cast area."

I sit down and check out the Lazy channels. Sure enough, there's a channel for the cast to discuss their projects. People are building robots, sticking paper together to see how big a tower they can make, making dinner for the homeless. Loads of projects, all sorts of stuff. I've heard of this sort of thing before. Innovation days to get ideas from the staff into the hands of the company, kind of like a great big copyright grab. Well that's how you might see it if you're cynical. But I'm not, of course. Winky fucking face.

"What are you working on, Vasi?" I ask.

"Oh, nothing really. Just this game thing." I like that they're humble. He's pointing at what looks like an ancient computer motherboard that's he's wired up to his screen and keyboard. "I'm trying to get this going. It's gonna be sick."

I study his face. I don't think he means 'sick' in the way I might mean. I inspect his work. "Looks like an old Commodore 64."

He looks at me with shock in his eyes. "Yeah. How'd you know?"

I laugh. "I know all about these things. You'll be telling me next you've got Defender going."

"No, but that's first on my list."

Berry hovers behind us. "Are you coming to kick off, Vasi?"

We all troop down the stairs to the Cast BDD kick off in the atrium.

Today and next Monday are the two days in the month when we can choose to do any project we like. Anything. The only condition is that we have to tell everybody about it at the session at the end.

I think about this. What can I do, if I can do anything? I have to say there is something exciting about the idea. What could I do?

I let that thought sink in while I listen to Amber present the projects that are starting up today. Tattooed people in T-shirts and skinny jeans climb on stage and present their work, ask for help, explain where to volunteer if you can lend a hand; that sort of thing. Amber then bangs on about humans being allowed to be Sweet Fucking Awesome and being given the freedom of expression and a whole load of hippy shit. She explains how Sweet has got more value out of these two days than out of any other stream of work and that the cast should all be proud. *Yay! Jazz hands.*

I suspect she's talking directly to me. She gives me that ravenous Alsation stare, particularly when talking about Sweet behaviours. I got the links for those books she'd been talking about and immediately assigned them to the email dustbin. Am I interested in *The Culture of High Performance*? Or *Embracing Chaos to Weed Out Seven Dysfunctions*. No, I'm not.

And I'm not surprised that Sweet thinks it gets more value from these BDD days than at any other time. My lot don't seem to do anything for the rest of the time, but come in early just for this. It's not that they get more, it's that nobody does anything else.

I see Freya standing a few rows ahead and to the side of me, waiting to go up to the front. I smile. She smiles back. My stomach churns. She's not wearing such revealing clothing today. Just the Sweet FA T-shirt with *Cast Champion* emblazoned on the back.

Amber explains how the cast champs are there to help with anything today. Ordering pizza, bringing round sugary treats, dishing out coffee and chocolate to keep us going into the small hours if we so want. The Cast Champs stand up on the podium and wave. They wish everybody the best-ever BDD. "Go back to your seats and innovate," they shout out. *Yay! Jazz hands.*

Interesting slogan. I'm reminded of the two Davids mounting their Liberal/SDP battle bus with a similar cry back in the eighties: "Go back to your constituencies and prepare for government." That didn't go so well. But times have changed, maybe this will go better, and I doubt any of the millennials in this room would get the reference. All told, I'm not sure I believe that letting people do whatever they want amounts to good business sense. I'm just glad it's not my money.

As we file out of the cast room, Freya grabs my arm.

"Hey, Jack. Can we talk?"

"Sure."

She leads me across to the other exit for the room and into The Wizard Of Oz. A large conference room. The lights flicker on as we walk in.

"Sorry about leaving so suddenly last night. I'd had a bit too much to drink. I thought it was probably time to go before it got messy."

Promises, promises. I relish the idea of it getting messy. I relish the idea of sharing another bottle of wine with her and maybe spreading some relish over each other. That dream and peeling off underwear and rolling on the duvet and licking and kissing before an inevitable sweaty denouement cavorts through my mind. I am well aware this is not the sort of thing that most men admit is going on in their heads, and I always wondered at what age it would stop. It hasn't stopped yet. Neither the desire nor the ability to act on it — I'm told that some men at my age have problems in that department, but while I have plenty of mental issues I do not, thankfully, have to worry about illness or slow degrading or atrophy or vascular problems or angina or high cholesterol, like so many men I know. But as I've grown older it is true that such explicit thoughts are more selective about who they are applied to. It's far rarer than it used to be for me to be worrying about giving much away in the trouser department, if you know what I mean.

But right now, I am suddenly aware of a stirring.

"Oh. It's okay," I say. "I think I'd had too much too. It was time to Uber." I mislead, because of course I'd stayed to finish the bottle.

"Can we do it again?"

Too fucking right. I can't wait. When? Tonight? I'm free. I've got fuck all to do because I've estranged my entire family and lost all my friends. You can take me out now, for all I care about BDD. *Yay! Jazz hands.* Now? Shall we? Let's go to my place and I can see what you've got on under those jeans.

But instead I say something much duller, like, "That would be nice. I'm quite busy this weekend. How about next Wednesday?" Next fucking Wednesday — what was I saying? Twat.

She looks a bit disappointed. "You're not free tonight? The BDD drinks?"

"Oh that? Yeah. Of course. Yes, I was going to go to that."

"Great." She touches my forearm with her fingers as she turns to go, and smiles. She's got a beautiful smile.

I get a phone call from Caroline as I'm heading towards my desk, and I dive into one of the sofa chill-out areas to take it. I'm not certain why I'm in a rush to take the call, but I've been on edge since Em ran out on me and I got the news of the pregnancy.

"We've got a big leccy bill this month. I'll need a bit more allowance," she says. I haven't even said hello, or indicated that I'm listening. She's just assumed ... she happens to be right, but that doesn't stop the cessation of pleasantries from annoying me.

And, I also don't see why I should keep supporting the family home. It's been nine months since I took my own place, and Em is working. But instead of acting like a grown up and making a date to chat about how we move forward or anything mature like that, I just go into a sulk and start disrupting from afar.

"That's *my* problem, is it?" I ask. I know it is, because that's what we've previously agreed, but hey, we've agreed loads of things in the past that suddenly don't seem to matter, like, I don't know, being faithful, forsaking all others — that sort of thing.

"Do you have to start now?"

"I'm not starting, you're starting. You asked for money. That seems like a start to me."

I'm very aware the sofa chill-out zone is not private. Sweeties are moving about the office, returning from the BDD kick-off and looking for places to hold their own chill-outs. I am trying to keep my voice down, but the way she asked for money has got my goat, so I am shouting a little. Not much. Measured. But if you were in the chill-out zone with me you would realise I was not actually chilled out. I wonder if there are rules forbidding this.

There's a long pause, I think I can hear deep breaths, and then Caroline says, "Jack. We were friends once. Can we just be friends?"

Caroline sounds lovely. Reasonable, calm. She sounds like she needs my help and support. Like she used to. Her voice is heartfelt, kind, sexy even. A low timbre with a gentle waver. It makes me sad. I want to hug her.

But of course I let none of these feelings out. I am very aware how Caroline's anger can become real and furious. I lock them down under a big black, fuck-off tarpaulin and put a comedy ton weight on it. Feelings-be-gone.

"We stopped being friends when you fucked video boy," I say. And I whisper it. I think that adds to the menace and hurt I want to express. And besides, Sweeties are sitting just near me on the other sofa.

"Can we get past that Jack? Move on? We've been friends since. It's not an unreasonable request. Let's do it for Em and our grandchild."

She really is being measured. I think she's thought about this phone call and planned it. I don't know why she started by asking for money, even though that was certain to rile me. Seems like her strategy and her tactics aren't working together. But she's reminded me of the baby and my resolution to sort my life out, and there are people within earshot so I start to soften.

And besides, I'm looking forward to being a grandparent. I think I might be a bit young, but then we started our family late. Despite meeting at uni and being faithful lovers for years, we didn't marry until we were thirty and only started trying for kids then. We figured kids could wait until we'd established our careers and had earned some money. Paid off the mortgage a bit. You know. I'm sure you get that.

But that means we have only just reached the point in our lives where the kids are leaving home, and guess what? Neither of them has. Em has never made enough money to rent anything other than a mouldy slum, and my son — well, he's just living in the wonderland zoo. No reality going on there; he'll never move out.

And yet Em is expecting my first grandchild. It's sobering and frightening — a bit; exciting — slightly; but I find the thought gives me enough focus to behave myself during a phone call.

"Okay, Caroline. Let's do it for the baby. What do you need?"

And suddenly, with those few words I feel a ton weight

lifting off the feelings tarpaulin as if it were an eiderdown of fluffy ducks. We even talk nicely to each other for a few minutes. We ask how we are doing and what work is like. I agree to go over to the house to fix a few things up. And I find I still like her. Love her, even. It's a longing and a sadness all rolled up into a great big sausage.

When the call ends the black tarpaulin floats away.

I'm smiling.

I feel good.

:-)

I spend the rest of the day helping Vasi. They're trying to get this ancient computer going so he can play their dad's collection of eighties games. Games with which I'm totally familiar. I remember *Lunar Lander*, *Frogger*, *Donkey Kong*. But most of all I'm desperate to play *Defender*.

It was one of those genre-defining games. Up until then so many games had been variations on the theme of *Breakout* or *Ping Pong* – let's face it, the computers didn't have enough power to do much more. Even though I hate to admit it, you can see the parallels between *Space Invaders* and *Breakout*. Instead of a bouncing ball going back and forth you have a missile launching from the moveable base. All you need then is for the wall of bricks to sidle from side to side. Two or three ideas to go from *Breakout* to *Space Invaders* and then into a whole range of games on the same theme: *Galaxians*, *Phoenix*, *Asteroids* (a stretch this, but I'm not getting marked).

But *Defender* was different. It's hard to see where the idea had come from, except the genius mind of a teenage programmer somewhere in Japan or wherever it was. And this was something that was so exciting back then. You had tiny little software companies springing up in dusty terraces up and down the country, building things that nobody had ever done before. A new medium that took maths, art, storytelling, problem solving and general knowledge mixed into a great big blender. You had kids my age writing tiny little programs and getting rich overnight because the programs they created were so phenomenally useful and nobody had seen them before. It was a gold rush.

"How did you get into this, Vas?" We've been soldering joints and trying to get the thing to boot up with a bit of success, but the image is temperamental and won't hold still on the screen. And then it's turning off periodically. We've been working hard together and the conversation has been about the work. This is the first personal question I've asked them – I think I have that pronoun thing right.

"My dad. He's about your age, I guess."

That doesn't make me feel great, but I let it pass. "He has good taste."

Vasi shrugs. I sense there's something they aren't saying.

"Do you get on well?"

"Not really." They laugh. A sad laugh. A laugh that has more in common with a sigh than a laugh. They turn to me. "He won't speak to me because — because of my gender neutrality."

I don't know what to say, so I say nothing. I think I might nod a bit and I might even mumble an "I see." But I'm most probably just silent on the matter. Vas, I suspect, is used to this reaction, because they pick up the oscilloscope probe and start checking the signal coming out of the CPU.

But I'm deep in thought. I take a seat on a nearby sofa.

There are two things on my mind. One is how I don't understand why Vasi's father wouldn't be proud of this lad — and I'm just going to pass over the gender issue for now. He's intelligent, thoughtful, kind — yes he can be a bit suspicious and passive aggressive, but that's just because of reactions to his life choices. They aren't choices I could make, and neither, clearly, would his father, but they are choices that should be respected.

"You okay?"

I look up and see Freya.

"Yeah. Err, yeah. Just deep in thought. Um …" She's staring quizzically at me. I sense she wants to ask a deeper question so I head her off. "Have you seen the work Vasi is doing?"

"They're fire, aren't they? A genius."

I nod. I remember the party. "Should be good tonight. I'm looking forward to it."

"Me too. See ya later." She's twiddling a gold necklace with a pair of slot-machine cherries at the end. She smiles as she turns to go, and I see the glint in her eye again.

Baked beans.

9

It's raining again as I get over to the family home about five. I still get a stomach twist when I approach the house and I'm never certain that I'll get a comfortable reception, even when I've called ahead or we've made arrangements, like we have in this case.

The house we bought ten years ago is a semi, three-bedroom affair. I think it was four bedroom when originally built, but at some point somebody knocked two bedrooms into one, knocked the dining room into the kitchen and added a lean-to extension on the back so you could sit under the rain without getting wet. It's the sort of house I used to think was a starter home, one to move out of as quickly as possible on the way to an old vicarage in a country village. If we were starting out today it would be well above our price range.

I ring the door bell.

My kids have no hope of buying their own place. Both of them live with Caroline, and with me having to pay rent in town we're really stretched. Em works for this NGO and makes next to nothing, and Oscar/Geronimo — well, who knows what a furry suit fetches these days. I don't see people queuing up in Sainsbury's for fox and rabbit onesies with liftable rear flaps, so I suspect the market is limited.

The rain makes this line of thinking more depressing than it might otherwise be. It's falling heavier now and is beginning to leak through the seams of my ten-year-old jacket. When I think about it, just about everything I own is ten years old. The house, my jacket, my car; I have shoes that are ten years old, my phone must be approaching ten years old and I swear I have a pair of Jockey Y-fronts that have been with me for ten years. And while whenever I put them on there is a comforting, homely kind of feel to things — supported in life, as in undercarriage — they represent some kind of failure. There's something round and repetitive about this number ten. Perhaps a little sinister.

I think back. Ten years ago we moved into this semi; the kids were fourteen and twelve. I had just left the job at Fergusons (a little while after Ted was sacked for the giant penis stunt) and life still felt like it was getting going. As if there were possibilities to be entertained and progress to be made. But now?

Caroline comes to the door in white painting overalls. I recognise them immediately, since we had his and hers overalls that we used to wear to decorate or do odd jobs around the house. Hers never fitted well and she had to roll up the sleeves and legs and put a belt around the middle. Her cleavage always looked great in a pair of work overalls. I smile.

"Hey." I look her up and down — I shouldn't, I know, but with the previous couple of phone calls and news of the baby, a thaw has set in between us and I'm much more relaxed. She seems to be more relaxed too. "You're looking good."

She smiles. "It's just the overalls, Jack. You always had a thing for these. I never mistook your lust for me in painting-wear as lust for me in general."

She's right, of course, but I don't want to show her what I'm thinking so I pull one of those dog-doesn't-understand-head-tip things and ignore her comment as if it's weird. Then I deflect with a question. "Decorating?"

"The bathroom ceiling. Cleaning out the cobwebs and giving it a fresh coat."

We pause. Just looking at each other with easy smiles across the threshold. Three decades of decorating history pass between us like a flash flood. I remember the flats we've painted and the baby rooms and the arguments over colours and the return of wallpaper and accent walls and the welcome demise of rag rolling and stippling. And I remember cute blobs of crimson paint on her nose and in her hair, and the urgent sex on paint-covered sheets when we didn't have curtains in the windows or carpet on the floor.

I imagine she is going through the same flood of memories as I am, and perhaps she is, but her thinking takes a different turn when she says, "Geronimo isn't in." She shrugs. "You've got time to pick up some of your stuff."

And that's sort of how it's been for three years since Oscar performed the great reveal one Sunday afternoon just before dinner and before we watched *A Bridge Too Far* for the umpteenth time. Our relationship simply cannot exist without the tension of his choice pulling us apart. It's aggressive, damaging, selfish, hedonistic, a choice an individual makes that has consequences for the lives of everybody else around, and yet the choice is made without consultation, discussion or preparation for the fallout. Suddenly the magic of the threshold moment is gone; we're consumed by furry madness once more.

"Still painful, Jack? When I mention his name?"

I nod. I think of Vasi's choices and his father. I say, "It's improving." I'm trying to convince myself.

"Come on," she says, "let's have a drink." She grabs my hand and leads me into the house. She sits me down at the kitchen table and opens a bottle of red. I watch her pour great big measures in tall round glasses. The action is warming and seductive. How nice it would be to just stay here.

"Here's to the baby," Caroline says, tapping her glass to mine with a chime. "We're going to be grandparents."

"We did something right with Em, at least," I say, and she gives me a reproachful look knowing exactly that I'm not saying how marvellous Em is — though she is, of course — but I'm really saying how awful it is to have a son like Oscar/Geronimo. I take a big swig of wine.

"He's not evil, Jack," she says.

"No. But he's not normal."

"Who is these days?"

I shrug and take another swig.

As if she's fishing for information, she adds, "What are the youngsters like where you work?"

I laugh. She really does have a point. Nobody seems to be normal anymore. In our early adulthood everybody strived to fit in — abnormalities were covered up, hidden, suppressed — for the sake of being normal. Now? Well, abnormal is the new normality. You can't fit in unless you're an outlier. I'm not for a minute saying it was good before, but you couldn't have lived your life as a teddy bear in the eighties.

"I don't really know how to start describing them," I say. I laugh some more, take a swig more wine — actually, I finish the glass and Caroline reaches over to pour me some more. In that moment, as she concentrates on the bottle, I look at Caroline and marvel at her beauty and at her calmness. She's got these stunning grey eyes that suck me in like miniature whirlpools, and gentle lines in her face that soften and blend her expressions.

"Give it a go," she says.

And so I do. I explain Sweet's culture and its emphasis on giving people total autonomy to do what they want, and I talk about my team and how they spend most of their time sending miniature animations to each other over the internet and then branching off multiple conversations all going on at once so that nobody looking in can follow a single continuous thread of ideas or see that anything ever reaches a conclusion. I explain how in my first week I insulted a gender neutral 'They', pissed off a culture vulture, exposed my ignorance about social media and nearly got sacked for suggesting somebody was attractive.

By the time I've finished explaining the events during my week at Sweet, Caroline is laughing so hard I think she's going to wet herself. It's infectious. I start laughing along with her in between great swigs of wine. I'd forgotten how good it feels to laugh with somebody that you deeply understand, and how great it is to share intimate knowledge of each other's lives. If I said it was like putting on an old glove I'd be guilty of underplaying the significance and using a shit metaphor and a cliché. This is like making two halves of a watermelon whole again, or adding spaghetti to bolognese or shooting the spaceship in *Space Invaders* and getting three hundred points then taking out the last alien with a perfect shot. Somebody once told me that getting a dog was like filling a dog-shaped hole in your heart; a hole you didn't know existed. Mine and Caroline's love was like that. Until I met her, I didn't know the isolation I'd been existing in. Now we're sitting at the family kitchen table laughing, I'm reminded all the more of the pain and suffering we've put each other through.

"I'm sorry," I say. It leaps out of my mouth without any conscious control, as if I was being controlled by a grand puppet master. But once the words are out, taking them back is impossible.

Caroline stops laughing and her face hardens. I guess she'd forgotten herself too for that brief moment, and she knows my apology is more than just a veneer; it's an attempt to sum up the whole fucking mess, lump it together in a huge pit, cover it in concrete, label it *do-not-uncover* and forget it ever happened. It's fantasy of course. But well … there you have it.

She nods. "I know, Jack. I know. But this was never about you and me. It was about you and your rejection of Oscar. Why is it you can get on with all those youngsters at your work but you can't speak to Oscar?" She lets that question hang so it sinks in, and just as I'm about to answer, she adds, "You never really connected with him, did you?"

I don't know what to say. So much goes around in my head in a short space of time, but none of it comes out. There's a feeling that it's not fair because it's not just my fault, it's his fault too, but then I'm the grown up, so I'm embarrassed at my own failure as a parent. Then I'm sick with longing because I want to wind back the clock by sixty seconds and take those stupid *I'm sorry* words back. Up until that point I thought we were healing, going somewhere, back in control of the relationship and by extension, our lives — more correctly my life. And then there's a deep, deep layer of shame that Caroline knows I rejected my son and that — just perhaps — I rejected him well before Geronimo ambled onto the scene. What must that have done to him? Did I reject the fucking bear, or did the bear come as a result of rejection? Did I cause the problem? Did I in fact create the bear?

While I'm in turmoil, staring at anything in the kitchen

126

except Caroline and unable to speak, she moves around the table and sits next to me. She puts an arm around me. The sudden warmth of her embrace is enough for me to break the cycle of despair and turn to her. I see tears in her eyes. I feel the warmth of her breath. I nestle in. It's like being forgiven.

I try to kiss her.

"No, Jack." She stands. "What do you think this is?"

I stare up at her in silence. She's suddenly tall. In control. Has the moral high ground and strength. I feel weak in comparison. A child. Uncertain.

We look at each other for a while, her with a reproachful, but I think a slightly playful look — one that I'm not willing to test — and me feeling sheepish.

Finally I look away, pick up the wine glass and focus on taking another long gulp. "Did you have some jobs you wanted doing?"

"I think we can leave those for another time."

I get the hint.

"And Jack," she calls after me as I'm putting my coat on at the door, "you know there's no us, don't you? Not unless … you know."

I nod. I know. Not unless.

I spend most of the evening following my somewhat confusing visit to Caroline, shouting. But it's okay to shout when to do otherwise would mean you couldn't hear each other because of the loud music. I'm in a bar down the road from Sweet and nearly the entire cast is here, as far as I can tell. My team is here, at least, and they are hanging on various sofas and chairs thumbing devices. It's like they haven't left the office. Ted is with the other managers, my peers, in charge of the various departments. And I keep catching Freya's eye.

I meet the others, and of course everybody knows who I am because of the surprise introduction at the beginning of the week. In between the pardons and the sorry-I-didn't-catch-thats, and the many sentences I simply don't hear but can't be bothered to ask them to repeat, I'm quizzed half a dozen times as to what I think of my first week, and do I have any insights. They use the word *insight* as if it has some other secret meaning to the one normal people know about. As if somebody in alt-corp business has patented the rights to insight and you're not allowed to use it anywhere else.

I suffer a tedious lecture — I think he says he's in testing, or QA — I can't remember — about how Sweet is in the fourth stage of its transformation journey and has a growth mindset born out of an experimental, hypothesis-driven strategy. Really?

I ask, "Does the black box thinking prevent the swans from landing, or are we mitigating risk through *being* flexible or just *doing* flexible things?"

He purses his lips and thinks deeply. "Interesting. We'll have to catch up on that one," he says, before disappearing towards the bar. Tosser.

I have a drink on my own and then Ted wanders over. He's looking smart, and I've noticed him networking the room. Clearly it's my turn. After three or four drinks, I'll have to be guarded.

"Hi, Jack. I've been wanting to catch you but it's been a busy time." He smiles.

I smile.

"Now you've had a bit of time here, what do you make of the app? Got any insights?"

Really? You too?

"Ah," I say. I search his face, looking for tell-tale signs to suggest if he really wants to know or if he's just making conversation. I think of the giant penis. And whether that influences me more than the drink I don't know, but I suddenly decide to be frank.

"What it's doing is monetising things that we once didn't have to worry about because they were taken care of for us. It's given us more to worry about."

He stares. "What do you mean?"

"It's like this. We used to have a card limit and we had an overdraft limit. We set them once a year or every few years or when we changed banks and then we forgot about them. Sweet's app makes me worry about how much I spend on groceries compared to petrol, compared to gifts. I have to worry about what my kids are spending on and control it by setting up accounts and giving them limits. It helps me with suggested budgets for teenagers and students and tweens and stuff, and I'm given advice in the form of notifications when spending approaches limits and the messages guide me into the app and into the software to make further adjustments. I worry that I'm getting all this stuff wrong. I worry that I'm a bad parent if I don't do it. Forgive me, Ted, but this is not giving the consumer control, it's giving the consumer more to worry about."

Ted looks startled. He takes a drink of his water. "Why don't you undermine the entire business model, Jack?" He laughs. But I think he's seriously unnerved. Then he says, "You got any more insights?"

I hesitate.

I don't really want to keep speaking. But I can't not accept the invitation, if that's what it is...

Fuck it! "Just think of all the apps that fit this model," I say. "I set up an internet shield on my router to stop my kids downloading porn or watching R18s. My phone's always asking me to update for security reasons. We had a location service to see where the kids were at all times. I have an app that tells me to phone my mum every two weeks, or send my brother a birthday card. None of this is taking back control. It's being controlled."

Freya is standing next to me with her phone at the ready by the time I finish talking. She pushes her way between me and Ted. "Selfie!" she says and raises her mobile to the obligatory arms-stretched selfie position. We all smile. "It's one for the party channel."

"How do you think Jack's getting on?" asks Ted, shouting over the noise that seems to be hitting a peak.

"He's cool for an old bastard," she says, looking me up and down.

Ted nods. "Yes. Must talk later."

I seriously worry he doesn't mean it, and I watch him squeeze through the crowd towards Amber.

"I may have upset him," I say.

"Ted? No. That's impossible. He's lovely."

Freya looks at him admiringly. I hope she's right.

I spend the rest of the party in conversation with her. She shows me the photos she's been taking, and I mostly listen. I listen to what she has to say about Sweet and about her work, and as I listen, I drink. Rapidly. I get pissed, but so does she, and she asks no more uncomfortable questions about Oscar/Geronimo, which is a bonus.

At some point she tells me more about the house her grandmother left her. Some Victorian place on the posh side of town that must be worth a million by now.

"Grandma told me she bought it for just ten thousand. Imagine that?" She touches me on the forearm. "It's lonely, though. And it needs work."

I think her touch lingers just that little bit too long, and we're rapidly into baked beans and Walnut Whip territory.

I drink.

"I need a man to help with some of my plumbing. A bit of screwing needed too. The shelving's loose. It's so difficult to get men who know what they are doing."

Walnut Whip.

I stumble over my words. Part drunken slurring and part baked beans. "I'm pretty good with a power drill," I say.

"Naughty, naughty." She touches my arm again.

At midnight or just before, or just after, we get an Uber back to my place.

Perfect end to a Friyay.

10

I wake the next morning to a few realisations that creep up like a mantis playing statues.

Number one, Freya is no longer in bed but is up and about. I can hear her in the kitchen.

Number two, the sex was good. Not the greatest. Drunk sex is rarely that good, though it is often urgent. We were new at it — together at least — so that means we have yet to find a rhythm (and sorry for any uncomfortable imagery that word provokes). And it was urgent — mostly due, I think, to the excitement of a new partner — from the moment we got into the flat until we collapsed in a sweaty heap and fell asleep.

Number three, this complicates the situation at work. Not that I wasn't actively complicating the situation from the moment I told Freya she was attractive, but actually making love is something that tends to turn things more interesting. Not necessarily bad, this, but ... complicating.

Number four, I've not seen Em since our little confessional. Em has a habit of just turning up, and I'd rather she didn't appear while Freya's here. Then again, I'm supposed to be the grown up, aren't I?

And number five ... my bladder is full.

I get up, shrug on a dressing gown from the back of the door, visit the bathroom then join Freya in the kitchen. She's found a white sheet and is sitting at the table with it wrapped around her. I assume she's naked underneath. She's thumbing her mobile phone in the way young people do. I've found the propensity to use thumbs to use a mobile instead of a finger increases the younger you are. People of my generation tend to use an index finger, and while my kids, Freya and the millennials (that sounds like a band) use their thumbs — which to me is ungainly and difficult, like trying to kick a ball with my left foot or writing left handed. I marvel at the speed of her typing.

She looks up. "Just letting everybody know I'm no longer single." She smiles. She's beautiful. Dark tussles of hair fall across her shoulders and her blue eyes shine even at this time of the morning, and even after the considerable amount of wine she consumed not ten hours earlier.

I shake my head; I doubt my eyes are as shiny, and my head needs some clarifying with drugs and coffee before I'll be able to hear or speak properly. "I missed that. Too early for me. Something about a single?"

She stands up and the sheet falls from her shoulders onto the floor. She walks over and drapes her arms around my neck. She stands ever so slightly on tiptoe and leans on me. She looks me in the eye. "I said, I'm just letting everybody know I'm not single any more. I've found a man."

"Ah." Though the actual utterance is mumbled as she kisses me full on the mouth. More of a "Amm–" I can feel the warmth of her body pushing against me and the kiss is insistent, pressured. Yes, it's nice. I even manage to respond so that she doesn't realise my mind isn't on the kiss but is thinking about the complicated bit that I'd been going over in bed.

She pulls back. "Nice. You taste lovely in the morning."

Forgive me if I'm cynical about this, but I'd had a skinful of wine, probably didn't brush my teeth last night and haven't yet this morning. I can't quite remember all the details, but drunk sex often includes mouth-led activities beyond just missionary intercourse and rolling over for a good night's sleep. None of the above suggests to me that my breath and oral sanitation are going to be lovely this morning.

But no matter. The male is the male, and the next kiss she plants on me leads to a fuller response and so on and so forth until we are back in bed replaying the night's activities. If I'm honest, I'm quite surprised at my resilience. I'm able to cope well, she seems happy, the sex is more relaxed, takes a bit longer (I think), and we lie there together for half an hour before we attempt to get up again.

At some point during the 'lying there' I venture to ask, "So, who are you telling about not being single?"

She rolls over towards me and presses the full length of her body against mine. "Everybody, of course. Everybody on my Instagram and Tumblr feeds."

Holy fuck, this is awful. I know we've had sex and everything, but I'm not certain I even like her yet. Sure, I like her femininity, the way she looks and smells and the way she moves, but … well … I don't know who she is. What makes her who she is? I certainly don't know if I want a relationship, let alone tell anyone about it. But then if she chooses to tell some of her friends, I guess that's no different to me boasting to Larry in the pub about my new conquest and him telling a few of my other acquaintances. The wheel turns but remains forever still, doesn't it? Medium may be different now, but the results are the same, surely? No need to panic?

I decide to check.

"Everybody. That's good. You have a tight group of friends?"

"Yes." She laughs and pokes my cheek. "Don't you?"

"On my phone? Not really. I don't like it much."

She bounces up in the bed and kneels over me. "You don't like your phone. OMG. I couldn't live without mine. It's everything." She stares at me, not sure if I'm joking. "Really? You really don't like it?"

It seems I have unwittingly opened up a rich seam of interest. How do I get back to my original question? I shrug — which is quite hard lying down in a bed — but I think the intention is right. "No. Not much. A bit intrusive. I don't like being available all the time."

As if on cue I hear a 'ding' from the bedside table.

"That's the first response," she declares. "Let's see what they say." She picks up her phone, reads the message then shows me the screen. "GFY babe. SYL. *Yay!*"

What the fuck did that mean?

"I don't know who that is," she says. "A friend of a friend."

"You don't know who it's from?"

"No. She must follow me. Cool, huh?"

She says these words excitedly while bouncing slightly on the bed.

I'm beginning to worry. "I thought you'd only told your close friends."

"Yes. Everybody who's following me. I've got over a thousand followers. They all want to know what I'm doing." She studies me for a moment. "You're not following me, are you? This is going to be so much fun. I can be your teacher. Where's your phone?"

"Hang on, hang on." I'm laughing as I say these words. The thought of being her pupil for a bit is appealing, I must admit, but I don't really think the imagery going on in my head is the same as that in hers. She's like a toddler suddenly, but I'm horrified that everything I now do is being broadcast to the world. A thousand followers that need to be fed and watered. Really. What are they doing with their day? "So they're not friends?"

"Yes. They're my friends. They're everybody. Family, old school friends, people from work. Most people at Sweet follow me."

That rush of shame rises again. It suddenly feels very cold under just one sheet and with half my body out of the covers. But she seems utterly unconcerned that she's just declared herself to be in a relationship at eight twenty on a Saturday morning, having spent most of the previous work-do evening talking to me. Thank fuck she's not yet said who she's in a relationship with. I've seen these things — my daughter had a string of teenage crushes and sweethearts that she dutifully declared on Facebook — big a few years back, if you remember — and it was just a matter of updating a status to say 'single' or 'in a relationship'.

A 'ding' interrupts my thinking.

"Here's another. It's from Berry at work. 'Hi Babe. *Yay*! [Jazz hands]. Send a wave to Jack.'" Freya waves at me.

I feel sick. "How about we have some coffee?"

I watch Freya operate her mobile phone while I sip coffee, make breakfast, clean up a bit, put the radio on, listen to some news. She responds to the ding of her phone instantly, like it's attached to her hand. She can be in sentence, half-way through a mouthful of scrambled egg, listening to me as I put in the occasional comment — whatever she's doing she stops to pick up the phone and respond with a double-thumb whirr of activity. It's impressive, in an isolated, thinking-about-human-skills kind of way. Like how I used to think it was impressive that the winner in *Crackerjack* could balance Monopoly on top of teddy bears on top of basket balls on top of magic sets etc.

etc. all while packs of cub scouts cheered and yelled and the presenters ran around shouting and laughing. It was a skill. Useless, but still, a skill.

At some point, though, I start to think about asking her to leave. I'm smarting from everybody at Sweet knowing my intimate movements, and Freya's microscopic attention span is beginning to annoy me. Actually, that's not fair. Her attention span is terrific, it's just that it's limited to answering dings on her phone. I wonder if they are all even from real people or if she's just answering the automatic answers of a thousand Google AI bots. It seems a funny thing to get excited about. But what do I know?

Besides, I'm worried about Em. While Freya checks her phone for the hundredth time, I check mine once to see if Em has responded. This needs to be sorted out. If I can't get her on the phone today, I'll have to go up to the house. I can do it. Oscar/Geronimo might be there, but Em needs me. No. Scrub that. I need Em. I'm going to be a grandfather.

"OMG is that your phone?"

"This?" I stupidly hold up my phone.

"No wonder you don't like using it. How old is that thing, anyway?"

She reaches over and takes it from me. She thumbs it a bit while I explain I've had it more than five years, it seems to be doing all right. It does what I need. She completely ignores my dialogue.

"Who's Em? Is that your daughter?"

"Er. Yes."

"Sorry, I didn't mean to be a nosy cow," she says, and passes the phone back across the table.

I get the impression that being a nosy cow is exactly what she intended. In fact, it seems that prying into other lives is all this generation seems to do well. When everything's out in the open and there to be inspected, what else is there to do?

"We need to go shopping," she declares. "Come on." She stands up and rapidly thumbs something into her phone. "Five minutes for the Uber. I've got to nip back to my flat, but I'll meet you in town."

She dashes into the bedroom while I finish my second or third, maybe fourth, coffee. When I follow her into the room she's spraying perfume onto the pillow. She shrugs. "Just leaving a calling card."

And then, within a couple of minutes she's thrown on last night's clothing and is out of the door to pick up a taxi from the pavement. She leaves with a promise to text a meeting point for some retail therapy.

To use her language, WTF have I got myself into?

I meet Freya after four or five text exchanges. This is her default mode of communication and I'm hiding my incompetence in this area so she doesn't realise (a) I'm twice her age (b) I'm not cool.

She's wearing a green anorak, which only reaches down to her thighs. It's cold out. There's a chance of rain and the sky is a miserable grey canopy that means summer's long gone and you can look forward to months of fucking awful weather.

"Hi, Babe," she says, pecking me on the cheek. It's odd. We seem to have gone from strangers to a committed relationship in the course of one work function, two shags and a cup of coffee. There's nothing cagey or tentative about her behaviour. She's just in it. In with me. No questions. I'm her boyfriend, and it's as natural a progression, to her, as del comes after ctrl-alt.

To me? Well. This is just fucking odd. I've had sex with

prostitutes and even tried a few proper dates since Caroline and I split, but I've not been in a relationship. I'm not actually sure I'm in one now, but Freya seems to think otherwise and I don't want to burst her bubble. It did cross my mind to just tell her to get out and leave me alone earlier this morning, but, well, I like her being around and am invigorated by the rush to make it permanent. That and the pressure of knowing she'd immediately tell her 1000 social media followers what a bastard I was — well, it was a bit sobering knowing that 300 of them are my work colleagues. Railroaded is a word that springs to mind, but I'm sure it will be fine and I'm enjoying being in the carriage. So she's twenty years younger than me. It'll be fine.

She buys me a mobile phone. Or rather, she selects one for me to buy. A posh one. It's a week's salary. I'm horrified. But when we upgrade my contract so I have unlimited texts and data — apparently I don't need to worry about voice calls because (a) nobody makes voice calls anymore and (b) they are included anyway — the cost is just over fifty quid a month.

She sends me my first text on the new phone. "New phone. *Yay*! Welcome to the 21st century. [smiley face, aubergine]"

I'm not sure what she's getting at? I'm a vegetable? And besides, I had a phone. It worked. I was quite modern, I thought, and I wouldn't be upgrading — so-called — if it wasn't for the promise of more nights like last night. And then I feel mean for thinking like this. I'm just going to go with it.

Over coffee, she tells me my image needs updating. The 'dad jeans' are apparently old hat, and the button-down collar could work but only if the shirt was checked, not plain.

We go shopping.

I like being with her, and it's flattering, being with a beautiful young woman and getting dressed up like a twenty year old, and I know I probably look like a twat with a daughter who's buying her dad presents, but … well, it feels good. It's a lovely distraction from the previous year and the disaster of family life.

The jeans she selects wrap around my calves like vices and the narrow turn-ups add an extra level of discomfort. I complain.

"Don't be so grumpy," she says. "You look great. We're missing socks and shoes."

I laugh. "I'm actually enjoying myself."

I suspect, though, that she's seen through to the grumpy core. And I am nervous of new clothes. I mean, I used to buy tight clothing and it wasn't uncomfortable. But when did I suddenly decide that clothes had to be loose and shapeless and hang like sacks from a washing line? I don't know. At some point just before or after the children were born, maybe. I try to remember the last time I wore tight trousers and I can't — except when attempting to fit into things I've not worn for a while, like my twenty-year-old penguin suit or those ski pants I thought were so fashionable.

But of course it's not just clothing that I'm grumpy about. It's everything. Traffic, housing, politics, Brexit, Trump, the EU, greenhouse gases, the internet, Facebook, Google, phones, attitudes, the young … fucking everything.

Yet Freya is lifting the bonnet on some of this attitude problem, and I'm seeing it for the craziness it is. Not that this is the first time. Em's been talking about it for years and buying me the odd T-shirt or pair of socks. I suppose the difference with Freya is that it seems so easy and not a chore. Em's so fucking earnest, and everything has to be organic and sustainable and with no plastic in it. When Em buys a retro top, it really is retro, it's original, it's being re-used and she got it at a jumble sale (okay, so she got it on some online auction thing, but you get the idea). Freya, on the other hand, is free. Maybe it comes from her being that bit older than Em. She's actually a different generation, a generation that grew up expecting everything, whereas Em's generation came out of the womb, saw how fucked the whole place was and is grateful there's anything left for them at all. But keeping the global fuck-up out of this for the moment (as my generation is so good at doing) Freya is helping me to steam clean the engine, and it needs a shitload of cleaning.

We go to the shoe shop next. You've probably guessed what happens. Yes. Plimsoles. I buy them. A hundred and fifty quid. They are red with white flashings. What we used to call go-faster stripes. They are a super-popular brand of footwear that I've never heard of. Crazy Shark, or something. Freya knows all about them and talks to the salesman about the various options. I keep out of it, but I know this is too much money to be wasting on impressing Freya. My ears burn with worry as I tap in my credit card PIN number. I justify the expense of everything with the expectation of my first paycheque from Sweet and a resolve to stick with the job. And I won't be buying anything else new for some time.

And then it's colourful socks, T-shirts with, apparently, the latest ironic memes on them, and then a haircut — shaved close up the back and sides, longer on top and smoothed down with hair gel — product, in hairdresser speak.

It's a makeover, though Freya doesn't use these words until it's all finished and I'm standing in my new togs, holding shopping bags in each hand, and she's taking a photo. I worry I look like an old fucker dressed in his grandson's clothes, but she is reassuring and seems to find me irresistible. It's nice. Puzzling, even. What can I say?

When the shopping is all done and I'm dressed to Freya's satisfaction, we have a slice of pizza each at some New York-themed deli that I've never been in before. The pizza is three foot across, smeared with tomato sauce, mozzarella and those shrivelled, slightly burned, slices of mushroom. As we eat, Freya uploads the photos to her social media accounts. I'm nervous. I don't really want her to share this stuff, I think it's private, but at the same time I'm curious. I mean, she thinks it's normal. I tell her I'd rather she didn't share so much.

"You sound like my gran," she says, and laughs.

I take a bite of pizza. "Your gran? Where are your folks?"

"I'm an orphan."

This is a surprise. I haven't met many orphans in my life. I don't know what to say. "Ah. I'm sorry." Pathetic, really.

"It's okay," she says. "I was only seven. A car accident. I don't remember much of it. My gran brought me up. Just round the corner, actually. Where I live now."

She takes a bite of pizza and I look into her face for sadness or regret or some sort of emotion, but she seems to be just eating a pizza normally, like everybody else. A bit of mozzarella stretches from the corner of her mouth to the table and she pinches it off between her thumb and forefinger, with a grin. I suppose this is new information only to me.

"You live with your grandmother?"

"I live in the house. Grandma died a few years ago. She left me the house. She used to tell me all sorts of stuff about my dad. He had a clapped-out old car and was a champion swimmer. He even won a *Space Invaders* competition when he was a teenager. He was a bit like you, I think."

She takes another piece of pizza and I reach for some water. I take a sip. I don't say anything, but eat a slice with her. It's warm, sweet and chewy. We finish the remaining slices in silence.

"Let's get you set up," she says, pushing unfinished crusts away and reaching over for the new phone.

We spend an hour or more setting up various apps on the phone, creating accounts, signing in, signing on, completing little tests to make sure we're not robots (though why the thing cares, I don't know).

"What's your favourite movie?"

"*Star Wars*," I answer quickly.

"Really?" She actually looks a bit shocked. "OMG, that *is* like my dad."

I pretend I haven't heard the daddy reference. The daddy thing is worrying me. I stick to the film topic. "Serious question?" I ask.

"Yes. Of course, serious."

"Well, *Star Wars* is up there. You know, the original and best. But now. Um. So many good films." As I talk, I'm going through a hundred films in my head to find one I can call my favourite that she won't find lame. And then it occurs to me that trying to second guess the lameness or otherwise of a film as seen through the eyes of a millennial is a daft idea. On the one hand I could choose something old school, ironic, or post-modern, while on the other it could be sexist, misogynistic, genderist or facile. There's no way of knowing until I open my mouth. I discovered this with my children several years ago. The best thing to do is to choose something and stick with it.

"I love some of the Marvel stuff," I say. I do — well, love might be a bit strong. But it's okay for a fifty-something to like cartoon characters these days. In fact, there's a bit of class to it. I saw Jonathon Ross explaining his love of Marvel when the late, great Stan Lee died. Ross is an historian of this stuff, and if it's good enough for him, I reckon I'm allowed a small bit of it.

"Which character?"

"Spider-Man."

"Cool."

Test passed.

She begins thumbing my phone, and within moments I have a new ringtone and sound when texts come in. Remember that friendly neighbourhood Spider-Man song from the eighties? Well, that's my ringtone. And the text alert is a camera shutter. I think that's a somewhat oblique reference to Peter Parker's alter-ego as a photojournalist.

"How do you do that?" I ask. For the life of me I don't even know how to set the ringtone on a phone. I did once, when mobiles looked a lot like normal wired phones and the menu was all text based, but since then I've not bothered to change from the factory settings.

She shrugs. "Just use the menu. Follow your nose. Here …" She shows me the combination of screen swipes, pushes, pulls, pokes and taps that are needed to change the ringtone. "I downloaded the notification track from a media-commons website," she adds, as if it's the most natural thing in the world. She sends me a string of texts to make it sound like my phone is taking a string of rapid camera shots. She laughs. "That's cool," she says. "Sounds like you're a hot instagrammer."

I wonder how she can know all this and put it into practice, and still have time to do a day job and function in the real world.

By about three in the afternoon, I am a new man. New phone, new clothes, new hair and, it seems, a new girlfriend. I watch her drive off in an Uber and my phone immediately starts taking photos and vibrating in my pocket.

It's a picture of an aubergine. Several of them in a line, and a comment, "Keep up baby. Loving it. Boom. Sizzling. IWFUAS." I have no idea what she is on about.

It's inexplicable how the male mind works. Freya's gone and I'm immediately thinking about Caroline again. I'm filled with a sudden urge to show off my new look. To show her how far I've come and, if I'm honest, to try and make her fancy me like she used to. I might be an old fucker dressed up in millennial clothing, but I reckon I look okay. Compared to some, anyway. I call her on my new phone — after I've found the address book, navigated to her number, pressed on what I thought was 'call now' a couple of times only to have an 'edit contact' screen appear, and then had trouble getting back to where I was.

By chance, she's in town. We agree to meet up.

And as I sit in one of the numerous coffee places waiting for her to show up and inspect the premises, all the optimism drains away. The latte in front of me has a love heart in foam floating on the top and two small coffee beans coated in chocolate in the saucer. It is a coffee experience. The coffee menu above the counter sings the praises of a dozen blends and preparations. Latte for that comforting morning feeling, flat white for a mellow afternoon, mochaccino when feeling adventurous, americano when it's time for serious business, piccolo on the go, chai for those well-being moments, long black for a taste sensation and short black for an intense coffee burst.

While I sink into a well-being moment, I think about Caroline and, yes, I think about the bear too.

You see, there's no possible reconciliation between us while I'm not reconciled with Oscar/Geronimo. It's what she was talking about on the phone and she's made this point very clear in the past, through Em, but I've not wanted to listen. I haven't been able to. But there's something about Caroline's insistence that if I can cope with bearded Theys, vaping ADD programmers, tattooed twenty year olds and teams of flip-flop-footed designers, I should be able to cope with my son in a bear suit. Perhaps she's right. Perhaps it's time.

She arrives and she's with Em. From the bags they're carrying, I guess they've been shopping, and I notice Em is in what I might call 'normal' clothing. The leather jacket has been replaced by a mac — unmistakably from the vintage collection in the attic — and as she removes it and drapes it over the seat, I see she's wearing a pair of blue maternity trousers from the same collection. I'd recognise them anywhere. They are an evocative reminder of sleepless nights, fear, anxiety, pain, and gas and air.

I go to the counter and buy them both a mellow afternoon — which at two-eighty a pop seems like a fucking bargain.

"What's with the new look, Dad? You look great," Em says. She seems genuinely excited for me. "Doesn't he look great, Mum?"

Caroline is altogether more suspicious. "You got a new girlfriend?"

"No, of course not," I blurt out — probably too fast.

Perhaps I should have gone along with it first in a jokey way, but my mouth is already ahead of me "You know. Just fancied a change. To go with the new job. You really think these jeans suit me?"

Em laughs. "Sooo much better than your old dad jeans. You could have put two of you in those."

Caroline smiles.

"I hope that means you think I look slim," I say.

Caroline laughs. Em laughs. I think the danger of her intuition catching me out has passed with the self-deprecation and humour. I congratulate myself on my quick wittedness. And, I suppose, I'm hopeful the new look does indeed make me look a little slimmer. After the initial anxiety, it even makes me feel good. I realise that feeling good about new purchases puts me, for the moment, in the camp of fashion victim or advertising fodder or unthinking consumer. I doubly realise that these micro endorphin rushes you get when buying stuff is exactly the sort of un-reconstructed, primaeval response from the lower regions of the brain that is turning the planet into a hothouse and our children into social-media slaves, but you cannot doubt the power of it. Oh, the irony!

Caroline sips her mellow afternoon and says, "I liked the dad jeans." She shrugs and looks me in the eye. Her laughter lines give away the humour she's trying to hide behind a dry exterior.

"Mum … you're so lame sometimes."

"Now, now. Don't call your mum lame. She's entitled to like dad jeans. Much the same way as you're entitled to like elastic-stomached maternity pants."

"Dad …"

We all laugh now, and we start talking all at once. I realise we're behaving like a real family. Like we used to.

Casually teasing, effortlessly passing information about what we've been doing and how things are going and what our plans are. I'm careful to keep Freya to myself, so have to edit my words by thinking ahead a little, but otherwise it's an hour of joy on a dark October afternoon. We drink the coffee, have a slice of black forest gateaux between us (though Em takes the largest share without apology) and the conversation settles into planning for the birth and baby clothes and car seats and all the other verbal paraphernalia that goes with pregnancy.

"What are you going to call him?" I ask at some point after the cake has been reduced to a smear of cream and chocolate on a white plate, but the question is waved away with a tut and the conversation continues between Caroline and Em.

I sit and listen to most of this with only the occasional comment, and my thoughts turn to Oscar/Geronimo. I realise that Caroline and Em have been equally guarded in their conversations; also editing their thoughts because I'm quite certain one or both of them would have mentioned soon-to-be-uncle Geronimo if I hadn't been there.

This is no way to be.

"Can I say something?" I interrupt the discussion on the evils of disposable nappies.

They both look at me, waiting, no doubt with a pinch of he's-only-a-man salty cynicism, for some additional nappy wisdom. But I surprise them both when I say, "What would it take for me and Oscar to mend?"

11

Over the next week, I get a few knowing looks from the team and my peers but nobody talks to me about the social media storm Freya has set off. And I know that she has, because my phone has been making photo noises and shaking and telling me I've got notifications for something or other. When I look, they all seem to be responses to Freya's responses to other responses about, well … about me. After a while I ignore them all, but I've been unable to turn them off. I'd be more disturbed if anybody was paying attention. But, nobody seems to care.

Nobody, that is, except Amber. She's clearly after my dinosaur hide to make into a chaise longue so I try to avoid her. And that seems to be okay. And she's easy to avoid. Except when she comes up to my floor on the hunt.

"I need to speak with you, Jack. We might have a problem."

And she takes me off into a side room and checks that I'm adhering to Sweet values, and wonders if by having a dalliance (she uses this word, I don't think I've ever heard anybody use it in real life) I might not be treating people sufficiently Awesomely. We discuss it. I want to say that sharing orgasms is exactly the kind of Sweet Fucking Awesome team-building that most of us enjoy.

Instead I nod with concern and talk about being consenting, single adults.

And it is consenting. At least a few times during the week, I've consented. It's great. It's going okay. Yes, the ever-present device is a bit annoying, but I'm feeling refreshed. Almost happy.

Relationships with the team are going all right too, and they are certainly not being sullied by me asking any dirty questions like "How's work going?" or "Have you done that thing for our stranded-with-no-money customer on the Isle of Wight?" No, as warned, I consciously avoid talking about achieving things and let the team tell me what they are working on and why — if they want to. I don't press it. I don't want to give Amber any ammunition and I don't want to incite any more complaints.

It makes me wonder what the point of my role is, so I take the time to listen in to conversations about the work and understand more and more about what makes Sweet tick. And the thing is, it really seems to have done very well just trusting its staff to get on with stuff that they want to do. No direction, no instruction, just a general desire to do something useful for the good of the company.

And then on an unseasonably sunny afternoon, I'm pulled into an emergency so-called product meeting. Most of my peers are here, as well as some technical folk, and of course Ted and, licking her lips, Amber. She catches my eye early on. I'm uncomfortable.

Some issue with the software needs to get fixed. I have to admit I find it hard to follow the conversation, but the drift is something like: "Customers are not enjoying the tariff selection experience because the account on-boarding experience, on which it is dependent, has developed a latent feature which filters Sweet Pay clients."

When not at work or seeing Freya, I've been preoccupied with family matters and I've been taking advice from Em about how to handle the coming meeting with Geronimo. For a start, Em has convinced me that I must only use the name Geronimo and that part of accepting my son for who he is will be to accept his chosen name. The name still sticks in my throat like I've tried to eat a two-hundred-year-old Native American headdress, but over the week I've become more used to the idea. We've agreed to have a meeting over wine and cheese at the family home, as if it's some sort of seventies key-swapping party. Oscar — I mean Geronimo — will feel at home in his *den* and I have agreed with Em and Caroline that I will listen. I won't speak unless asked a question, and under no circumstances will I offer an opinion on anything. Nothing.

I've agreed to Em's terms and Geronimo has agreed to attend as long as Em and Caroline are with him. Fair enough. I don't want him growling around without some moral support myself. But as the date has neared I've become increasingly angry about the whole thing. I want to normalise relationships, but how can I have a normal relationship with a grown man who wants to eat sugar puffs for an evening meal and have his stomach tickled as a greeting?

Tonight's going to be tough, and I still have to get through this meeting.

Customers are ringing in for help and the Liaison Agents are being overwhelmed.

We listen to a tape.

Customer: It's not working.

LA: Which experience have you selected?

Customer: I don't know what you mean by experience.

LA: What's your account tariff?

Customer: I think it's about three pounds a month.

LA: Yes but what tariff is that?

Customer (now getting irate): Like I said, three pounds a month.

LA: Please open your account settings.

Customer: How do I do that?

LA: Click the little spanner in the right-hand corner.

Customer: But it's only small. I'm not sure my finger can click on the right hand corner of the spanner.

LA: Caller, are you on a mobile device?

Customer: Yes, I can move it.

LA: No, are you on a phone or a tablet?

Customer: Yes, I'm on the phone.

LA: So in top right corner of your phone is a little spanner–

Customer: The top right corner of my phone has a disconnect symbol. But your website has a spanner on it. What do you mean?

And so on and so forth. As we listen we laugh. But I am taken with the tragedy of it all. The whole thing is full of misdirection, misunderstanding and error. The man sounds like he's in his fifties, just like me. He seems to know a bit about computing, but not much. He's afraid of getting it wrong and he doesn't understand the language.

It could be a set up, a comedy show about the 'computer says no', except we listen to call after call of the same sort of thing. The customer simply doesn't care about the way Sweet is carving up its clients into demographic accounts or options or tariffs no matter how much they are told of the benefits, or services or Fabulous Friyay Offers they are missing out on. They don't care because they are over it. Too many offers, too much choice, too much time spent fucking around with the mobile phone in your hand when you could be picking your arse — which at least has some sort of pleasure associated with it.

People are fed up with it all. It might be okay to have one application fail because you need to renew a password, but when you have fifty all clamouring for favours, updates, notifications, authentications, messages, settings, choices, account management, etc. etc. it's beyond human endurance. At least for somebody my age.

And I wonder if this is how it's going to go? Are we old fuckers destined to spend our senior years isolated because we simply cannot access things anymore? I worry I'll gradually remove all those essential apps until I can no longer do anything. I can't order shopping, can't get a taxi, can't buy things, can't keep in touch with friends, can't watch TV, can't watch videos, can't buy tickets for the cinema. I mean, I won't even be able to order a chicken tikka masala. What a fucking awful future I have to look forward to, if absolutely everything is monetised online or else … well … or else fuck off, you can't have it.

"We must get a grip on what the customer wants," Ted pronounces.

This sounds sensible, right? But what if they don't want what we offer? What if really, now they've seen what 24/7 mobile internet brings, they would not actually vote for it given the chance?

Ted continues to address us about the need to make our Experiences error free. "This mistake has cost us several hundred thousand, and possibly more in damaged reputation."

But I'm tired. I'm tired of the corporate bullshit and the delusion that customers actually want what is being pumped into their homes and offices.

So I say, "Can't we just use straight talk?"

"What do you mean?"

"Well. Why does everything have to be an experience? It's stupid. An experience is something exciting that you save up for, or you get once in a while by pure fluke. The heart races, the mind fizzes, you tell your mates, you share it with others. This, whatever this is, is not an experience, it's a chore. You do it because you have to save money or because you're going to get a penalty or because it bothers you until you engage with it. This is not an experience any of us really want. As an experience, it's a failure."

I might have tipped a bowl of lemon and salt down everyone's throats for the looks I'm now getting. You see, there's an unsaid law for alt-corporate businesses that you have to be optimistic and positive. Criticism, if it exists at all, is for peer discussion around behaviours and outcomes. Nobody is allowed to say something is a failure.

Amber shoots me a look as if I've finally revealed my true dinosaur colours. She's practically glowing with happiness, and I can see her sharpening the demi-gorgon claws. Or Dracula teeth, or hound of Beelzebub (insert your favourite horror creature here).

But I stand by my comments and feel myself swelling with nostalgia. "Computing was never meant to be like this. It was an enabler. It was good for stuff. Good things that we'd been unable to do before. It didn't make you so fucking confused with a thousand different log-ons that you had to register with just one media account to manage everything, and it didn't harvest all your sensitive information and sell it off to the highest bidder or some bare-chested Eastern European tyrant. It was a force for good. Good for people to be productive and good for companies to control their accounts and, yes, good for playing *Space Invaders*. Look at what we've done. We've created a parasite on top of a parasite on top of middle management."

"Really, Jack," says Amber — she shouts it, actually. Then when everybody has stopped being sick from the lemon and salt she adds in a quieter voice, "Thanks for your input. We have a problem to solve here and now. Hopefully by the close of play. Going forward, we can revisit the use of the *Experience* metaphor in a later marketing meeting *with the marketers*." She stares at me with the eyes of Cujo. "I'll take an action point to catch up with you about it. On me."

With those words, said so expertly with the exact right emphasis for patronage, she's fucked me right over in front of all these people. She's made me look as small and brown as the coffee stain on the table in front of me.

But then I shouldn't be surprised; I opened my mouth before knowing most of them and loudly pointed out the bleeding fucking obvious.

I'm not finished, though. I tell them they're stupid and wasting their time. I tell them they'd be better off going home and tinkering with their genitals for all the difference 'experiences' were going to make, and I tell them their flow-inducing, nudge capability for system-design thinking is a crock of shit. I say, Sweet FA really is Fuck All use.

Well … that's what I say in my head.

Actually, I say nothing.

Amber pushes her teeth deeper into my flesh with an, "Is that okay, Jack?"

And I nod.

I just nod and go silent.

I stare at the coffee stain. I might even start to pick at it with my fingernails. I imagine the Jack bashing is all over.

But it's not over.

Amber says, "But Jack, we need an explanation. Why has this happened now? This is your team's work and they've created a disaster. Did you review the changes before they went in, and did you make sure the team followed protocol for these very risky stories?"

Amber is holding pages in front of her. The whole group is looking at me, and I feel the shiver of cold saliva run down my back as I realise she has been getting this ambush ready and I just went for the bait. The truth is, I don't even know what changes she is referring to.

"Um. That's the team's responsibility," I say. Rather lamely, actually. I wouldn't be convinced by me if I was watching from the other side of the room. I feel the room stretching out in front of me, like I'm looking at it through a fisheye lens.

"You're the manager, Jack."

So suddenly I'm no longer the Squad Master, spiritual guide, cultural ambassador, but plain, old-fashioned, gantt-chart wielding manager with wringable-neck responsibility.

That's convenient.

I sit there and I take it, because I know that if I do otherwise it's show over. The show might be over anyway, but I take comfort in the small irony that Amber is not fat, even though she is currently singing. But I'm going to ride this out because I can, and until the HR department or Cast Champions or whatever come for me in a dark cloak with a scythe, I'm simply going to carry on. The millennials in my team don't give a fuck about deadlines and authority; why should I?

But I am embarrassed and angry, and after the feast, I seek out Freya to see if she has intelligence to add. I have to wait for a couple of hours, because she's in some meeting or other discussing the next Sweet social. I can tell this because I'm getting better at using the calendar tool Sweet has on all the machines. It tells me Freya is in Casablanca for the next hour, and when I bend down to look under the obscured glass, I can see she's with a couple of people I don't know. So I 'ping' her an IM on a Lazy channel to ask for a 'catchup' and she pings right back saying she'll come and find me, 'Perhaps for a drink? I'm thirsty. LOL'

I often get the feeling I'm missing subtext, but this sounds good. I could do with leaving early, a couple of calming wines and then off to the great reconciliation with Oscar — I mean Geronimo. While I wait for her, I search through the customer complaints records for a bit of a laugh. And a laugh is what it turns out to be. Sweet has customers that can't access the app, that lose their data, that can't make payments, that can see other customers' account information. Fuck me, it's a mess. I look at the dates and they're relatively recent, so this is an ongoing situation. Despite the headline figures of customers joining Sweet at a record rate, they are also leaving at a record rate. The salespeople (well, the digital marketers, I guess — nobody has salespeople anymore, they have social media manipulators and fake news generators and if the real world is lucky, they might just have an advertising team) are failing badly.

When Freya comes and finds me and we wander out to a local pub, all these moaning customers are still on my mind.

"Why are there so many unresolved complaints?" I ask.

"I know. It's a real problem. I heard Ted talking about it with the head of marketing."

"I'm surprised he still has a job."

"She."

"She. Yeah, of course." It's funny how often I'm falling into the gender arsehole trap at Sweet. I'm not getting used to it. This has not been a problem for me in thirty years in the workforce, but suddenly I'm slipping my tongue into the cavity of righteous indignation with every few sentences. But I'm seeing that it is at least my problem. Why should I assume the head of marketing is a man? And why shouldn't people get offended when I make that assumption? "She seems to be making a right fuck up of it."

We talk about Sweet's problems and I guess I rant a bit. We sit drinking for forty minutes and I finish the bottle almost all by myself. I'm probably slurring too, but I'm enjoying putting my theories across.

"I don't think the software is up to the job it's promising. Jesus, I mean, I can't think of the number of things I've tried that simply don't work and yet the product's been put out there to test the market."

Freya's swiping the face of her phone with her thumbs.

"My daughter got me to digitise all my music. I got an iPlay account or some other childish type of brand name thing that I had to keep in 'mySongs' in 'myComputer' in 'myDocuments' and downloaded 'tunes' …" I use air quotes in abundance in this sentence, but Freya's not really paying attention and I'm preaching. I know I am. I just like doing it, and I persevere; the wine's going to my head and with Freya simply ignoring what I say and rubbing her digits across a screen, it's like being with my kids again and I get into a complaining groove.

"I ended up with this digital library of all the music I could possibly want. But when I go to play something after a day at work and while I'm drinking a glass of wine, I have to turn the computer on, wait for the fucking thing to boot up, start up an app, authenticate using a password, reset the fucking password when it runs out or it chooses to forget it periodically, for reasons known only to itself — but I suspect it's so I have to go to the fucking password reset page which gives them a chance to sell me more stuff. Then I have to search for the music I want. Holy fuck. You'd think they would get that bit right — the selection of the music to play. Probably starting with the music you played before because that's usually what people do — you know, I've played 'Bat out of Hell' yesterday, I think I fancy me a bit of Jim Steinman. But no, it doesn't remember what you were doing so you have to start all over again.

"But let's assume there's still time to play some music after all this, and that the computer hasn't decided it's going to update itself. Now what am I going to play the music on? Not the fucking computer. That's like buying a sports car and using it to reverse up and down the drive. Despite all the stickers promising surround sound and — air quotes — authentic audio experience, any sound coming out of the speakers is tinny and pointless, and certainly not loud enough. So I have to plug the computer into the back of my amplifier, to get any kind of volume and quality.

"All this fucking software just never lives up to the billing. And that's the problem-loop that Sweet's software has fallen into. Overselling, under delivering, fix the fucking result and oversell it as if it's a new feature. Meanwhile the fix has resulted in a bunch of other fucking problems."

When I stop talking, I realise Freya hasn't listened to my fabulous speech. She's just been on her device and nodding.

She looks up. She smiles. "You need vinyl," she says. "It's the latest thing. But look at this, it's brilliant."

She shows me her screen. It's a couple of corn-on-the-cobs, one on top of the other.

"It's cornhub." She laughs and laughs. I've not seen her laugh so much before. "It's for farmers." She laughs some more.

I'm finding her irritating.

She rattles on for a considerable number of minutes. It's a combination of snorting laughter and repeating the word 'cornhub' and repeated swipes of her screen, and displaying more pictures of painted corn on the cob. I nod my head from time to time if it seems like I'm supposed to respond. I'm tucking into the wine and getting anxious and annoyed.

It's like being with Oscar/Geronimo and his annoying device habits.

I have to remember I'm the parent and that I've instigated the meeting. We've attempted meetings before. It starts with good intentions, a handshake perhaps, we sit down, and then it gets heated the moment one of us opens our mouth, because he's dressed as a fucking bear. I can't stand to think of my son as a ... what? I don't even know what you call it, does it come under the Rainbow umbrella? Is it the B in LGBT? Or do they need to add other letters to show acceptance of bears, unicorns, cats, mammals? LGBTBUCM — fuck, it's stupid. Maybe there should be a catch all — species indeterminate? Just an S? Or perhaps an F for Furry? LGBTF?

It winds me up so tight and so quickly I see red. I shouldn't. I know I shouldn't. It's my failing, you see. If I'd kept him away from the mind-polluting internet, got him racing Scalextric cars or shooting Airfix soldiers with a catapult, he'd never have discovered there was a community of Furrys out there because he'd have been too interested in the real, physical world. It's my fault. How can I blame him?

12

By six, I've had a skinful. I leave Freya sitting in the bar with a drink and her phone for company.

I wonder how long it will take for her to register that I've actually gone, but as I start walking my phone begins vibrating and clicking every few minutes. Freya is busy online sending me messages. I can sit with her for two hours and she barely speaks, then the moment I leave she starts sending texts. As each message arrives, my phone takes a photo — or sounds like it does. I try and turn the sound off, but I can't even tell which app is making it do what it's doing. There are half a dozen apps, each with little numbers on them. I think that means there are messages waiting to be read, but I can't be sure. Each time I click on one it takes me off to somewhere other than messages and I quickly get lost. I turn the volume down, as that seems to stop it making noises, but it's still vibrating in my pocket.

I walk — well stagger, really, I can't be sure but it seems to take a long time — across town to the family home. It's drizzling, but I have on a hooded jacket, courtesy of Freya, and I enjoy the cool on my face as I walk. I momentarily stop and look up at the rain. Ahhhh.

Freya's turning out to be annoying, but she's allowed me to spend some time and money on myself, to consciously be myself for the first time in years. I deserve to like me, and do stuff for me. I mean, what's the fucking point in leaving the family home if you can't do what you please? Really. I mean, I have some new clothes in my cupboard.

163

Not stupid presents I wear to please the kids — real grown-up clothes that make me feel human.

I'm inexplicably confident as I stumble past my car in the drive and reach the front door. I'm standing tall, proud. I feel good; wet and good and I can feel water dribbling down my face from my fringe — yes, I'm a bit wobbly, true, and I'm having difficulty reaching for the doorbell — it keeps moving — but nothing I can't handle. I feel as good as I have for ten years. Fucking better. Yeah. *Sick*, Vasi might say. I've a new job, a new girlfriend, I look good. Smart, tidy, on the verge of success for a young, ambitious firm that's going places with me as manager. Yes, fucking, yes. I am Sweet Fucking Awesome. I think this whole marriage, kids, house, car, Y-fronts business has been holding me back for too long. I'm a new man. My family will see that and we can reset relationships on an adult footing. Live and let live. I don't have to do all this reconciling on their terms. What am I, a man or a mouse?

The door opens. I almost fall in but hold myself up against the door frame.

I look up.

It's a giant bear.

It says, "What the fuck do you look like? New girlfriend bought you some clothes? And you're fucking pissed."

This is not a good start. He says 'new girlfriend' like he knows about Freya, and apart from the sheer hypocritical nature of the comment about *my* look, I am stunned by the ferocity. Is this how far things have degraded that my son can't even answer the door to me after being prepared by Em and Caroline?

And then I feel predictable, ashamed, as if I've just turned fifty and brought a shiny red sports car to drive to the golf course and back on a Saturday morning. A walking cliché. New girlfriend, new haircut, new skinny jeans. But as I introspect and begin looking at myself, another side of my mind, the aggressive, drunk male side gets defensive. Who the fuck does this giant bear think he is, lecturing me on my look?

"You can talk," I say. "You're dressed up like Winnie the fucking Pooh on an outing through the Hundred Acre Wood. I'm fucking sorry I forgot to bring the honey with me. Maybe you'd like to ask Piglet to pick some up from Eeyore."

"You can't accept that I am happy. You never could."

"Yes I can."

"You think so? You can dress up like a hipster but you're a fucking dinosaur lost in the seventies and you can't find your way home. What the fuck can you ever understand about being happy?"

"I could be happy if–"

"And even when we give you a chance, you fucking blow it. We let you near and you hurt Mum again."

"Don't fucking interrupt, I want–"

"Think we don't know about Freya?"

"What? Let me say something. What about Freya?"

He's shouting over the top of me. I'm shouting something about it being none of his business and I have the right to a life outside the family, but he's so busy shouting I know he's not hearing my shouting. "Stop fucking shouting."

"It's all over Facebook. Your girlfriend is a social media cliché."

I'm having difficulty focusing. The giant bear is like some sort of loud swirly animal dream.

Geronimo holds up a phone showing a selfie of me and Freya. "Here she is." He scrolls through a dozen of them.

He paws air quotes: "She's in a relationship with a man just like her father. You fucking pervert."

He slams the door in my face.

"Open the door," I shout. I manage to find the doorbell and keep my finger on the button in case, if I take it away, I won't find the bell again. "I'm not a pervert. *You're* the fucking pervert. Fucking bear. Fucking growl at me, go on. I'm fucking happy."

Of course, I'm not fucking happy, am I? But there we have it. That's how it is with my son. That's how it's been for several years now, and it's why, ultimately, I had to move out and why I should never have agreed to this meeting. I couldn't cope with his choices, and when he found out I'd been playing away he cut me out with a severity I couldn't combat. Even as Caroline and Em began to forgive and forget, Geronimo grew larger and Oscar grew smaller.

It was my fault.

I keep my finger pressed on the bell and push into the door.

"Open the door," I repeat, over and over. "Open the door." With each repetition I get quieter, and I get lower until my finger slips off the bell and I slip down the front of the door and collapse in a damp heap.

Eventually, I lose track of time, so I don't know how long I've been there. Cars have driven past on the road because I've heard the squelch of wet tyres in the rain, and I know the rain has become heavier because of the noise it makes hitting the porch roof. But at some point the door opens. I'm crying. I look up into Caroline's eyes. She's crying.

"Jack. You need to go," she says.

"But I came here to make peace. To mend."

"You're not helping. You're drunk. Nobody wants to see you."

"But Em. The baby."

"She doesn't want to know you."

"Please, Caroline. Please."

I suppose it's safe to say that my daughter is my rock. I know it should be the other way round, I should be the parent, but … well … I'm not. She's the sensible one living by values. I'm proud of her, but I need her.

"Jack. You don't need Em or me to validate who you are. It's obvious you can get along without us."

"Stand up, Jack. Get up. Be a fucking man, not an arsehole."

I'm not sure if Caroline is saying this to me or I'm saying it to myself. It's the sentiment I use when I talk to myself; judgemental, aggressive, the tough truth that nobody else dares say. Is somebody other than me saying it now? Have I finally been vindicated and found out after all these years of keeping it secret? I am a fucking arsehole.

I look at her through watery eyes. She looks like she's speaking, but I can't hear anything. She looks fierce, angry. She picks me up off the floor and helps me to my feet.

"Get the fuck up, Jack. Come on. Do you want everyone to see you like this? A loser grovelling at the door? You were more of a man when I met you than you are now. Get a fucking grip." I hear this demolition of my character.

"I can't," I say. "I've had enough."

"What do you mean, Jack? You've had enough." She's looking at me with utter contempt in her face. "You've had enough, have you? You poor fucking wretch. *You've* had enough." She's definitely shouting now. Shouting at the top of her voice with no concern for the neighbours — which was always one of her things. "Well that takes the fucking biscuit. After everything you put me and Oscar and Em through with your decade-long woe-is-fucking-me routine, you're the one that's had enough. Well go and stab yourself through the fucking heart with a knitting needle. I've got rope. Would you like some? Pills? There are fucking plenty here. All of us are on fucking pills, Jack. Take some, take the fucking bottle. I'll get them."

She disappears into the house, but is back in seconds.

"Here." She pours pills from a plastic bottle into her hands and then throws them at me. "More?" Again she throws pills. She's screaming and throwing.

I turn and walk away from the house, down the drive.

"You don't want pills after all, then? Too scary, is it? You're a fucking coward. Fuck off. Get the fuck out of our lives."

She goes back into the house and slams the door. I stand on the pavement staring at the house. Neighbours are at the windows on both sides and the streetlights have turned on, casting me in a sodium glow, sodden, in the rain with my skinny jeans wet and tight around my legs.

I watch the house for a few minutes. The porch light goes off and no other lights come on. It remains in darkness.

I turn and walk out of the close onto the main road. My family days are over.

13

I'm alive.

Where am I?

Not at home. Under a fucking bush.

I'm freezing cold, and soaked.

Oh fuck, my head.

Oh shit. Yes. The whisky.

I sit up and my head hurts like a demon.

I look about. Behind me is a tower block I vaguely recognise. A brutal concrete block, but I've been here before. Yes. Mandy. Yes — the pay-to-play girl.

What am I doing here?

I have little memory of the night after leaving Caroline's house. I walked. I found a supermarket and a bottle of Scotch. I walked some more.

And then I don't remember.

Jesus. The side of my head hurts. Unexplained Beer Injury (UBI). Though I think it's clear I was pissed as a cougar at an orgy. How I got where I am, I don't know, though.

"You all right, mate?" Some bloke has come out of the flats. He's in a leather jacket and jeans. He helps me up.

"Yeah. Thanks."

"You was making a right noise last night." He laughs. "I think you was singing that old Barry Manilow song. You know, 'Mandy', init."

Jesus. I grimace. "Thanks, mate. I'll make it from here."

I walk home. Slowly. I take care to put my feet smoothly

one in front of the other so as not to cause a shock to my head. Thankfully there are few people around before eight on a Saturday, and those I meet give me a wide berth. In any case, I'm too fucked up to care about it. I trudge slowly.

When I get back to my flat, I take a handful of ibuprofen with a pint of water. And immediately throw the whole lot up. As I retch, my head thumps like it's being hit with a full plastic carton of milk; the pain resounds like a giant bell going off in the fluid of my head.

I collapse on the bed.

And I dream. I dream I'm in a giant game of *Space Invaders*, and each one of the little aliens is somebody I've known and they're all shitting out missiles that rain down on me. They're using devices to remote control the missiles and fly them down. And every so often Caroline flies past in a spaceship and drops more missiles out of the window with an alien cackle. It's terrifying. I hide behind great green buildings labelled Reason, Truth, Harmony, Family, Reality. They're being bombed and turned to rubble by a procession of everybody I know passing over them, squatting down and taking aim. I'm screaming, *Leave me alone, Leave me alone. No! No! Noooooo …*

I wake. I'm in a cold sweat. It's some time in the afternoon but I can't reach my clock and I don't have the energy to sit up. So I just lie there thinking about the dream.

Like most dreams, it has some warped connection to what's going on my life — I don't need to explain to you — but I'm disturbed that this is how my subconscious is thinking about things. Am I really the victim in all this? The one being shat on by green-alien missiles emerging from the arses of my family, colleagues and acquaintances?

I don't think so. I am not blameless.

Talking of shit, there's a distinct whiff of dog poo about the place. I roll out of bed and find a dressing gown. I check my clothes, lying in crumpled heaps about the bedroom, and find the offending smears. It seems I have lain in some unsavoury-smelling muck and brought it back into the house with me. My skinny jeans are soaked through and there's mud and shit down one leg. It was a night not to remember.

By about four, I've been able to tidy a few things up, put a wash on, get showered and fry myself an egg on toast with a cup of coffee. I'm beginning to feel human.

The phone has managed to turn its own volume up because I've heard it take photos from time to time. I check my messages.

I have a dozen from Freya. Smiley faces, a few questions asking where I am, a few rolling eyes and then some grumpy faces, bunches of capital letters in seemingly random order. It's like trying to interpret the Rosetta Stone.

Then there's a message from Caroline.

"Are you okay? I feel bad. I lost my temper. Sorry, but you've hurt us all again. Who is Freya?"

I sigh. Fuck. Yes, she did lose her temper. She does that from time to time. This was quite a bad one, but not as bad as some of the others. She's thrown my clothes out of the bedroom window into the rosebushes before. She's attacked my possessions with scissors and she's changed the locks. This was all while we were together. So in the scheme of things, yesterday's carry on was mild.

Still, it hurt enough for me to down a bottle of whisky and spend the night under a hedge. But honestly. I don't know what to feel about it now. I'm numb. It feels like some sort of Rubicon has been crossed and there's no going back. Not just with Caroline, either, but with my son,

171

Oscar/Geronimo. Or whatever name he wants to be called now. Frankly that's okay with me. I've had enough of the fighting.

The phone makes the photo-taking sound. It's getting on my tits, so I pick it up to find a way to silence the thing once and for all.

Then I read another of Freya's messages.

"They're saying you lied on your profile, Jack."

Eh?

I reply. "Who are? What profile?"

"Where have you been? I've been trying to reach you?"

"Just at home. What profile?"

"Your Sweet one. The one we all liked. The one that got you the job."

"My CV?"

"No. The online profile. It's different to your CV. The one here." She adds a link to the text. I click it and a picture of me appears and a very modern-looking, immaculately presented profile renders itself on the screen. It's beautifully done. Nothing I could have created. I sound like a computing God. It's by somebody that knows me well, but who's left out all the bad stuff and put a PR gloss over everything. I know exactly who's done this.

"This is my daughter's work. It's not one I gave you. I sent in the CV."

"Nobody read your CV. Only your profile. They're going to suspend you :-0"

I laugh, thinking for an instant that this is a joke. But Freya would have put a winky face, not a shock face. She doesn't confuse her emojis and so I know this is serious.

If it wasn't for the hangover, I'd probably be more upset. As it is I have trouble distinguishing between the after effects from a bottle of Bells and the sick depths-of-stomach-churning that usually comes with news like this. I put the phone on the table with a clunk.

I sit staring at it.

It makes some photo-taking noises.

I stare.

It plays 'Spider-Man' and vibrates across the table.

I pick it up and throw it against the wall.

It takes a photo.

I walk out of the room and get into bed.

14

I don't go into work for the next week. I've been suspended. I haven't picked my Spider-Man phone off the floor and it's now stopped making noises because the battery must have run down.

Sweet's email came from Amber just after my last text exchange with Freya, and I could read it because I've got an old computer up and running in my bedroom. It's simple, one I understand, it does browsing and email and lets me muck around with code. And it doesn't keep telling me what to think. When I want emails, I start up an application and I ask for them. It doesn't try and do it all for me. I am in control of how and when.

Sweet are deciding what to do and I've been told to expect a follow up. Since my phone has died, this can only come via email, unless Freya turns up with a letter.

Freya doesn't turn up, though. Without texting and messaging it seems I am dead to her. It's as if I've hidden myself in a cave and rolled a giant stone across the entrance to keep everybody out.

But just because I've dumped the phone, that doesn't mean I haven't been busy. I have.

For the first few days after the family trauma, and then the suspension, I was so blue I spent much of the time in bed, and then, well, something just clicked. Like pressing the start button after depositing your ten pence in an Asteroids machine and waiting for a few seconds as it drops down the money chute with a satisfying thunk. I remember something Em said about needing joy, and I keep seeing the baby's crinkly book on the shelf by the kitchen window, and it makes me want to clean everything away and start again.

I start small, but important.

Instead of putting the skinny jeans in the wash, I throw them out.

I throw out the pink socks and the button-down shirt with waistcoat. I decide they aren't for me. That's right. *I* decide. Not Em, not Freya, not Caroline, not Geronimo and not Sweet.

Before long, I've gone through my entire flat and thrown out just about everything that doesn't bring me joy. I pick it up, examine it, determine if *joy* is the overriding emotion I feel when handling it and if not, it goes. Dumped.

I feel remorse when it comes to dumping the brand-new mobile phone, but this doesn't last. In the bin it goes, along with a ten-year-old pair of trainers and a tin of Tate and Lyle golden syrup from 1990. The remorse lasts ten seconds, perhaps a few more, and then I feel free and unencumbered by modernity. If I am to be labelled a dinosaur, if the name fits, then it's okay with me. Mr Fucking Brontosaurus. (And none of this revisionary Apatosaur nonsense either. A fucking great Bronto.) I have made the long-overdue decision to be my own man. I, on my own if needs be, am going to live my own life, and I won't be apologetic.

I have even thought about a new dinosaur-themed name for myself. I don't know. Barney seems a bit trite. Dino? Nah. Jurassic Jack? Lol. That's got to be it. I will look unkindly on any person that does not use my new dinosaur name properly and the pronouns it/they.

Okay. So perhaps that's going too far — I'm a dinosaur,

after all, and they don't take kindly to change. Maybe in time it will become a nickname ;-)

When it comes to throwing out the old computer I've been hanging on to for more than a decade, I baulk. It nearly gets taken to the tip, but then my joy evaluation remembers what it was like to be programming a computer for the first time. To be solving endless crossword puzzles in C or Assembler or Pascal or Fortran. Simple unfettered languages that solved real problems that people actually wanted to solve.

So I keep it.

I set it up on the kitchen table and turn it on. It still fucking works. Imagine that. It's not been made obsolete by endless updates or deliberate sabotage. It doesn't even ask to be updated — it doesn't even know it's out of date. It just actually works and the email client still connects.

I am in awe. Full of joy. In that moment the rock of my cave begins to roll back across the entrance to reveal a blue, sunny sky. I swear I hear the 10p hitting the coin stack.

But all the joy cannot stop Freya from turning up in my head, so I drop her an email inviting her for a drink.

I'm going to dump Freya. But funny as it may seem, I've never done such a thing before. As a teenager I was always the dumpee — usually prior to anything interesting happening — and with Caroline it was a mutual loathing of each other's behaviour and a fucking great bear that did all the damage.

I sit in the same bar where we had drinks those weeks before everything went to shit, waiting for her to turn up, a glass of water and a packet of salt-and-vinegar crisps in front of me. It's early so there are only a few punters, but I know as soon as five o'clock ticks over it will start to get busy. I'm hoping there will be a few more customers so that

Freya isn't tempted to start spitting and fighting.

When she turns up she's wearing the same Sweet FA Cast Champion T-shirt she was wearing the very first time I saw her, except this time I feel no baked beans or Walnut Whip trembles within, just a factual appreciation of a lovely-looking young woman and lovely person too, but not one I can continue a relationship with.

"Hey."

"Hi, Jack. You want a real drink?" She points at my water.

"Ah. No. I'm fine with this."

"Not thirsty? No drunk sex then?"

I laugh. A bit of tension dissipates. "No. Not today."

She raises her eyebrows then says, "I'll just … um …" She points to the bar and I watch her order a glass of some brown spirit and a can of Red Bull. I occurs to me that I should be buying, but that seems so baby boomer, so I sit on my hands — feeling uncomfortable.

I don't know how to start this conversation and I begin weakly when she sits down. "How have you been?"

"I've been texting. What's happening? You're ghosting." There's an edge of annoyance in her voice. "I thought about coming over, but then I thought if you don't want to see me, well … what the fuck. I'll be a badass mofo. I'm cool yo."

I think this means she's not going to spit and fight. I can't be sure. "Ah. Okay. I've been, you know, busy sorting things out. Family." I shrug.

She nods. "Your wife?"

"No. Not Caroline. No." I laugh, a sort of a laugh, more of a snort. "Me. I've been sorting me out. I've had some time to think."

"To think about us?"

"Yes."

"It's not going to work is it? Cancel." She draws a finger across her throat.

That's disturbing, but she's smiling — sort of. I shake my head. "No. It's not working out." Phew. I think that's done. The finger thing was just an affectation. I think. Well, that was relatively easy.

We hold a twenty-second silent vigil for the lost relationship, and Freya doesn't even pick up her phone. Then she reaches for the tin of Red Bull and pours half of it into the spirit glass, mixing the brown liquids. She takes a deep swig. "God I love this drink. Want to try?"

I shake my head. "No thanks."

She checks her phone. "Have you heard anything from Sweet?"

"Not yet. But I don't suppose it will be good."

She nods. She takes another deep glug and looks over to the bar. "Ted thinks you're great," she says.

I'm surprised. It seems unlikely.

"He's been asking around."

"Did you say good things?"

"Yes, Jack. Well, it was good, wasn't it? While it lasted." She flashes a cheeky smile.

I think back to the encounter and there's a momentary flash of Walnut Whip in my head, but it dissipates when she picks up her mobile phone and reads a message. She thumbs a response.

"I've got to go. Only time for a quick one. Pre-loading. Going out tonight." She downs the rest of her drink, finishes off the dregs from the bottom of the can of Red Bull and leaves.

It's over.

I'm left with my water.

15

I'm summoned into work at some point later in the week and I walk in under a cold blue sky. I'm in by 8:15 a.m. for the 9 a.m. meeting, and I go up to my desk. I don't turn on the computer; I don't even sit down. Instead I invite Vasi to one of the sofa areas for a catchup. They look like they've been in since the crack of dawn. They're wearing a rainbow shirt on top of black combat trousers, and their beard has been trimmed.

"Looking smart," I say.

"Thanks. We've been getting on with stuff. We haven't missed you."

There's no emotion in the way they say this. But I think it's a bit cruel. I don't say so. But I'm not surprised. They've (as in all the team, not just Vasi) heard about the "lying on the CV" and I start to explain myself but quickly stop. It's not worth trying. It will all come out.

I just shrug. "Bit of a misunderstanding," I say, implying Sweet have misunderstood, but actually I mean that me and Em had a misunderstanding. Vasi doesn't need to know the nuance.

It turns out she did a fantastic job of the profile. So fantastic they gave me the job on the strength of it without reading the rest of my CV, and just as well. The way Em told it, I was the coolest soon-to-be-grandfather this side of Siberia with glowing experience. But it was so full of inaccuracies, the truth was bound to come out in the end.

I don't mind. In fact I love her all the more for caring

and trying.

I talk to Vasi a bit more about my resurrected love of programming-in-the-old-way on old machines and I tell them about my new project — to code *Space Invaders* from scratch, just for the hell of it.

"That sounds fucking awesome," they say.

We laugh. "Yeah. It is."

We have much in common.

I get into Casablanca and sit down a few minutes before anybody arrives. I'm prepared to be sacked. That's fine. I've come to terms with it. It's not the first time. Though that fact wasn't included in the profile, which is what has caused the problem — well, that and other inaccuracies. I'm not going to defend myself. My daughter created the profile with the best of intentions, and while I wish she'd talked to me, I know that had she done so I'd have forbidden her from doing anything.

"Jack. How's it going?" It's Ted, the penis-drawing boss of me. He comes in to the room smiling and holds the door open for Amber, who has a rather less friendly look on her face. In fact she looks like a thundercloud on speed — if you can imagine such a thing.

I say I'm doing fine and that I think the team are going well.

He nods, listens, and puts his arms out on the table, weaving his fingers together. "You see, Jack, I have a problem."

Here we go. Dinosaur-skin ottoman coming up.

I say, "I know. If it helps, I'm sorry this has happened. There was no intention to deceive."

Ted smiles and puts his hand up to stop me. He shrugs. He actually shrugs. That's unexpected.

Amber grimaces, on the other hand.

Something's going to happen that I'm not prepared for.

"The company's in trouble, Jack." He stares at me. Is he going to blame me? I mean, I've not been great here, but I'm not responsible for everything.

And then he begins a rant. "We're not making our commitments to the customers and progress has slowed to the point that we're going backwards. Customers are leaving for — well, we don't even know where they're going because we're not collecting the metrics. But they are leaking from our platform like shit from a Victorian sewer. Whenever there's a release of new software we seem to create more problems than we solve. We have a list of faults as long as the Brexit negotiations, and I can't get management reports out of the system because our own security forbids me from logging in ..." He carries on in a similar manner for a few minutes.

I sit listening to the litany of problems he's facing as if I'm hearing myself speak. The sense of déjà vu is overwhelming and I have to stifle a small smile. Amber, on the other hand, is making the best of it by nodding along, but I know her rabid instincts to attack are being held on a tight lead.

"It's like you were saying at the BDD party, Jack. You really got me thinking."

Ted goes on for some considerable time. He explains that although Sweet is making money, they are losing customers because the software isn't doing what customers demand, and new companies with copycat products are nibbling at Sweet's heels. He says that a new approach focusing on delivering things people really want is what's needed, and all the nicey, nicey cultural stuff is great when you're not staring down the barrel of failure, but they can't afford to employ people just to make each other unfailingly happy.

And then he ends with a plea. He says, "I really need your help, Jack. It's why I brought you into the company, and it's time I set you to work. I wanted you to join because you have a record of cutting through the bullshit and saying it how it is. I've seen you operate and I know the managers you've worked with. And I've been impressed with your insight. Can you help me?"

Before I begin asking what he really means and firing my thoughts at him with both barrels, I stop myself. The thing is, I've had this type of request before. You get a mid-level manager wanting to know how it is and when you tell them, you end up getting sacked because the first thing they realise is that you are implicitly criticising what they are doing. This exact scenario is one I've been getting into in the last ten years at every single fucking job. Having seen it all, I've become horribly cynical about how companies operate, and as I've got older, I haven't cared too much who I offend.

I ask carefully: "I thought you had little to do with me getting the job. I didn't recognise you, at first. Sorry."

He smiles. "I thought not. It was like this. Amber gave me your CV and told me you have a great profile but that she'd noticed you'd worked at Fergusons where I'd worked. Amber takes it all in. She knows everything. Because she knew a bit of my history she was worried that you were making your profile look all modern and relevant when in fact you were a has-been trying to chance your way in."

Heaven forbid.

"You see, I did read your CV. Unlike anybody else. I took one look and realised who you were. And the thing is, Jack, we need some people to shake this place right off its shitty foundations, winkle out all the crappy nonsense and get people working at the right things. What you said about experiences and politically correct office spaces made me realise."

But I am surprised at how Ted brought me on board, I thought it was Amber — who is now clearly regretting it — because of my online profile and my modern attitude. In the end she had little to do with it. She must have hated me from the start. But another reason I'm surprised is because of all this focus on the company culture of Sweet Fucking Awesome and letting the chickens run the coop. It seems that Ted thinks, just as I do, that this turned into a great big crock of chicken stock mixed with heaps of guano.

"Here's a test for you," says Ted. "The company has a funding deadline in two months. If it fails, we're toast. You can have anything you need to make this happen. But you just have to make it happen."

I start thinking about the things that need to change. That fucking IM Lazy thing for a start. Then there's all the crap about *Sweet Fucking Awesome* and letting people please themselves. And the lunch breaks and the innovation days and the sitting around on sofas. I am going to get this place working, no mistake.

"Are all the owners on board with this, Ted?"

He nods. "Sure."

He seems certain enough.

"Well, I'm in," I say.

I realise that I'm not the only one thinking that skinny jeans and the apps on expensive phones and the texting and the TLAs and the emojis are wasting everybody's time.

I cannot wait to get started.

16

A few weeks pass, and I throw myself into work. Everyone agrees to ditch IM Lazy in core hours, and to check emails only three times a day — when they arrive, at lunchtime and before they leave. We police the working-from-home policy, the pet-therapy days and the duvet days, so that they're not abused. I even get agreement — with a few exceptions — that mobile phones are not for work, they are for private calls only. I reinstate desk phones for those that want them. I'm the most unpopular Jurassic Jack this side of the Pleistocene, but it suits me just fine.

I see Freya in the office most days and we are the best of colleagues. She's lovely — irritating, yes, and the Walnut Whip infatuation has gone. She was always way too young for me, and actually, I miss Caroline more than ever. I try not to dwell on it.

I get on with work.

Then one Wednesday night, when I get home at about eight, Em's there, sitting on my sofa drinking water and watching the news.

She stares at me. "Bad day?"

I must work on my posture.

"Office stuff. But okay otherwise. I thought you'd thrown your key away."

"No. I tried texting but you haven't replied."

"I've given the mobile up. You can just come round. Or call on the landline."

She swivels her eyes in the universal signal of madness

but otherwise ignores these new facts. Em engages as if nothing has happened in the last month, as if the brief estrangement between us was nothing but a loose thread in the otherwise flawless fabric of father-daughter relationship.

I sit across from her in the armchair. I loosen my belt. "How are you doing? I can see my grandchild." Em is showing even more now. Quite considerably, actually. She's wearing those jeans with the elasticated waist and has a frock under her usual leather jacket. I don't mention it.

"Months to go yet. He's kicking."

This is a magic moment in any loving pregnancy.

"He?"

She nods. "I think so. Can't be positive at this stage, but …" She tails off. She wants to say something.

I remember when Oscar's scans first showed a tiny willy nestled between his legs. We were so happy, so excited. Rivers of joy. That was when we thought we were going to have a boy — not a fucking bear. Shrug. Anyway, I won't go there now. That was an exciting day. I had all sorts of plans. Scalextric, Meccano, Lego. This lad was going to have the biggest fuck-off Lego set *in the world* (add Jeremy Clarkson impression here). And we did buy those things, but they didn't get played with except by me. I let the thought drop. It's not good for me.

"Have you forgiven me?" I ask. It's a simple question. I'm sure she's going to say yes, I'll hug and kiss her, feel the baby kick and we'll share a glass of water or push the boat out and have cheese and biscuits or whatever craving she needs to fulfil.

But she says, "I might. I have something more to ask."

Here it comes. Em is never far away with her suggestions as to how I can improve my life by getting back together with her mother, and I don't put it past her to suggest it now, even despite recent history. "Em–"

"No. It's not Mum," she says. "It's Geronimo."

Oh fuck. "Em, we don't get on. It's pointless. Even if I accepted him, we don't have anything in common. It's like asking a nun to date Beelzebub."

"And who is the devil in this scenario, Dad?"

"It doesn't matter. Nothing will make them have a cosy dinner for two at Heavens Above pizza emporium. They'll just fight. Try to convert each other, the other guests will hate it and…" I run out of creative ideas for this one, so I just dribble into silence.

"Dad. I want it. I want you to see Geronimo. I want you two to be civil to each other and talk."

"Even if I agree, he won't."

"He already has. Me and Mum have asked him. He said yes."

"Remember what happened last time?"

We stare into each other's eyes for a moment. She's silent and I'm questioning. When she fails to say anything after a few seconds I shrug, get up and walk to the kitchen. I open the fridge, take out a bottle of soda water, and I'm about to pour a glass when I see Em's face.

"I've stopped drinking," I say. I've come a long way in the month since the fight, even if I say this only to myself. Out loud I say, "I don't miss it." That could be a half truth. This is tough. I'm working on it.

She smiles. It's a smile that delights. All toothy and broad and cuddly. I walk to her and hug her.

"On my territory. My pub. Not at home this time, at The Flying Pig. One non-alcoholic drink and no bear suit. And I call him Oscar," I say.

"Dad. He lives to be Geronimo."

"Okay, Geronimo, but no bear suit or I don't do it. No

chance. Final offer."

She shrugs. "I'll see what I can do," she says, as if she's doing me a favour. And then she smiles. It's as if she already knows this will happen.

We talk some more and I bring up the topic of the father, but she's non-committal and determined to take utter responsibility for the baby without a male presence. She says that she had a fling and got pregnant. She didn't mean to, exactly, but she didn't mean not to. She's happy.

And I'm happy for her, even though I'd be happier if I had met the dad, liked him and knew he had good prospects and would look after my daughter. What an old-fashioned fucker I am. Em doesn't say that but I see it written in her smile. It's okay. I get it. It's not like it was.

But later that night I get a phone call on my landline and Em gives me a date and time. Oscar has agreed. Whatever way I look at this it's progress — it's good for Em and the baby.

And terrifying for me.

I get to the pub before Em or Oscar. Larry is polishing glasses in his usual place and a few punters sit at tables down the far end of the bar. Larry nods, takes a fresh glass from the rack above his head and begins to pour my usual IPA.

"A soda water with lime tonight, Larry. On the wagon." I pat my stomach in to say "I've overdone the pies."

Larry says nothing. He's a professional. He switches pulling for a button-operated dispenser, fills up a pint of soda, adds a twist and places it on the bar. He steps back and resumes polishing.

I take a sip. It's good. Not like the angry bitters I've been used to for thirty-five years, but things have to change. Anyway, bitter is an acquired taste. At first, when you're a teenager, you think beer is fucking horrible, but of course you can't let on. You persevere because of peer pressure, and then some day in your twenties, maybe later, you realise you actually like it. More than that, you actually crave it. I suspect it's some kind of response to masochism kind of thing that if you do something long enough — whatever it is — eventually your body gives up detesting it, moves into *I-can-take-it-or-leave-it* mode and finally decides you can't do without it in the same way you can't do without water or oxygen. I got used to bitter; I can get used to soda water.

People love all kinds of weird shit. You only have to surf the internet for ten minutes to realise that they must have gone through hell and back before beginning to like the perverted and disreputable — not to mention illegal — stuff that they get into. And what gets me is they film themselves doing it, and tell the rest of the world (that voyeurism-by-proxy sort of thing) that it has become commonplace. I mean, I wonder how long it took Oscar/Geronimo to decide he actually liked dressing up as a bear?

Some lads come in. They're already drunk and it's only 7:30 p.m. Must be a work do celebration of some sort. I smile as they go past, nod my head — in the language of pubs and drunken lads, that's an 'I'm no threat, but I'm also not to be taken for a twat,' kind of nod. They're dressed in button-down shirts and trousers. Smart looking. Probably work for one of the call centres around here.

I swig half of my water in one go and catch Larry's eye as he serves the lads who, at that moment, cheer. They're looking towards the door, and waving.

Without properly processing the jeers, I think I know

what's happening. But I don't want to believe it. I'm afraid to turn my head. Larry is looking up and smirking, and he's motioning me to turn around. I know what I'm going to see before I move, and Larry confirms my deepest fears when he says, "Sorry, mate, no collecting for Aunt Lucy in here," to a great roar of laughter from the lads.

I don't turn; I pick up my pint tight in my hand and take a cool sip. I don't know what I'm going to say. I don't know what I'm going to do. He's defied me. He had a chance for us to have a simple drink and chat down the pub like grown men, and he brought Geronimo with him. In person, despite our agreement. I am sad, and sick, all at once.

"Hello, Jack," I hear.

Larry looks shocked. "I told you, we don't do charity collections in here."

"I'm not collecting. I'm with my father." There's a hint of venom in the word *father*. Just a hint.

I put my head in my hands and nod slowly. "It's my son, Larry."

And then I hear, "No fucking bears in here, mate." One of the drunk lads has swaggered down the bar. He's feeling hard enough to take on a cuddly toy.

I turn to Geronimo. "This is what you fucking get. I said no bear. You agreed."

And then it starts to get all shouty, and I'm not certain who is shouting at who or in what order.

"I didn't agree."

"Oy! No fucking bears."

"It's none of your business, son. Leave it."

"What's wrong with fucking a bear, twat head? You want to try it?" Oscar turns and bends over.

"You've got a son?"

"What the fuck was that?"

"You a fucking poof bear an' all?"

"Sit down and keep out of it. We don't want no trouble in here."

"Is it Rupert or Yogi, you fucking bender."

"Leave it alone. Go back to your mates."

But his mates are now all gathering around us, pints in hand, menace in eyes — along with huge amused grins.

Geronimo does a little dance.

"It fucking dances."

And then Geronimo takes a lunge at the guy with a great big furry paw. The guy steps to one side, pulls Geronimo's paw and smashes his pint glass over Geronimo's head as the bear goes down onto the floor.

A couple of them begin kicking Geronimo while the others empty their pint glasses on him.

"Smash the fucker."

"Destroy it."

"Go on Benny, do him."

Geronimo is surrounded in a melee of kicking and laughter and beer spraying and shouting.

I feel this tremendous anger and fury, and suddenly I'm in the middle of it, flailing my arms and kicking shins, and stamping and shouting. I'm not sure at first if I'm defending my son or joining in the beating. I take a swing at some head or other and it must be one of the drunk lads, because he's standing up and isn't wearing a bear suit. The punch connects to the side of his head and I feel a sharp pain shoot up my arm. I land a kick on some bloke's knee, and he goes down on the floor with scream.

I hear smashing glass and shouts of, "Keep out of it, you old bastard." But I keep swinging and I connect my blows to two or three of them before I see a fist come at my nose in slow motion, like I'm watching a train plough into the buffers. I hear a sickening crunch and my vision is instantly veiled in orange and red.

I fall on top of Geronimo, face up. I'm surrounded by black shapes and blow upon blow is raining on to my arms and legs. My anger is directed at the bear beneath me and at the lads all around me, but I can't get up. I'm frozen on top of a fuzzy lump.

I catch a glimpse of Larry charging along the bar at the group with his famous baseball bat. And my last thought is how I'm quite proud that I've protected my son. But honestly, I think if Geronimo had been on his feet when I joined the fight, I'd have probably taken a swing at him too.

And then it all goes black.

17

I wake up in a hospital bed. I have random memories of an ambulance, nurses, flashing lights, inquisitive faces — including a bear — policemen and people being carted off swearing, but no coherent timeline on which to peg things. It's like having a basket of washing and no clothesline, so I'm left with this damp soggy pile in my arms wondering what I should do.

I have some pain in my head and ribs. Pain I can feel but which doesn't bother me. It's dark and the lights are down low. I'm woozy. But I feel safe. And quite content, actually. Also a bit floaty, without too much to care about. Slowly, I think I put together the story in my head, but it takes until dawn and it could have been hours or just minutes. I don't know.

At some point somebody opens the blinds and the lights come on. But I miss it actually happening, and when I open my eyes I can see another patient across the room from me. There's just two of us. He's sitting up drinking tea and he's got a great stitch line going across his cheek. Red and raw. It looks nasty.

He sees me looking and nods. I wonder if he was one of the lads in the bar. Maybe. I don't care right now.

I hear him mention something about tea and when I open my eyes again there's a nurse with a cuppa in front of me.

"How are you feeling, Mr Cooper? Here's a nice cup of tea for you. I've put a sugar in."

He helps me sit up, and checks my eyes. "I'm going to check your blood pressure," he says.

I am a doll. He manipulates my arms, puts a cuff on and watches some machine pump air into the cuff, then reduce the pressure, then pump. It's like some sort of demented timer, but at the end of it all, he seems satisfied.

"Doctor's doing a check in half an hour and you'll be okay to go."

"What happened?"

"Oh. I've only just come on. I'll get somebody to come and talk to you." And he disappears, never to be seen again.

I strike up a conversation with the man in the bed across the way, and he tells me we're in the A&E holding area. Not serious enough for a real bed but kept in for observation. He fell off his bike and hit his head.

"You look like a bit of a mess," I say.

"Thanks, mate. But you should take a look in the mirror."

And that's the first information I get about my injuries. The other data I put together tell me I'm not in serious peril, I've probably cracked a rib because breathing deeply is becoming more painful, and I've likely been sedated to manage the pain and keep me from moving too much. These are guesses, but at some point Em is shown in. She kisses me and smiles.

Then she sits beside the bed.

She laughs. It's a concerned laugh, but a laugh nonetheless.

"You think this is funny?" I say.

"You look terrible. But you're okay. I'm relieved. It's going to bruise, though. You'll have a couple of awesome black eyes."

"Don't use that word."

"Which one?"

"Awesome."

She looks puzzled but lets it lie.

I feel my face. It's a bit sore and I have dressings all over my nose and forehead.

"Is Oscar okay?"

"Geronimo. Yes. He's fine. He had padding." She shrugs.

It's funny. I laugh just a tiny bit, and the pain shoots from my ribs up my neck into my face.

"You got a broken nose and some guy's ring cut your forehead. I've been waiting all night. We were worried you had a clot because you didn't come round after being knocked out. They kept you under for a scan. The doctor told me it's all clear."

"I wish they'd bloody tell me something."

"Short staffed, Dad."

"What happened to everybody at the pub?"

"Geronimo says they all ran off rather than face the barman. The police rounded a couple up at the next bar. They didn't get very far."

"Casual boys' night out."

There's a pause in the conversation and Em glances over to the door.

"Dad?" she asks.

"Geronimo?"

She nods. "Can he come in? He's waiting outside."

"Sure." I smile. "Bring in the bear."

But the funny thing is, he's not dressed as a bear. He's just Oscar. He's shaved his light-brown hair on both sides and kept it heavy on top and swept back with a gel or cream or something. A hipster cut. I've seen dozens at Sweet. No full-beard though, he's clean shaven. Rings in both ears look a bit piratical and he's had his tongue pierced. But I just see a young man with pale skin, and worry in his eyes.

He's in T-shirt and jeans. Okay, so the T-shirt has a picture of Bungle from Rainbow on it, but I can handle a bit of light irony when dosed up with morphine.

"Hi, Dad."

"Hi, Son." I put out my hand and he takes it. He smiles. I smile. "No beard to go with that great haircut?"

"Beard's too hot in a bear suit." He smiles. He laughs.

It's quite sweet.

I take a few days off work to recover from my ordeal. Em, Caroline and Geronimo come over, and Geronimo is just Oscar. I see no fur, or overt growling and the bear suit is missing. I like to think he's stopped wearing it, but I know he hasn't. Every so often as he talks, I don't hear Oscar, I hear Geronimo. I've spent so little time with my son over the last few years that I never noticed he'd developed a whole affectation and way of being when he was the bear. He really did live to be that thing. I ignore these moments and bathe in the attention of my family without worrying.

There are probably more than a few reasons I am able to do this now, but not being at the family home stops me mainlining the old me, and stops me policing their behaviour. While I talk to you now, they're both flicking their phones, probably on some social thing or other. The telly is on, but Caroline too is flicking through stuff on her phone. Nine months ago this would have been enough to send me off at the deep end in a lead-lined submersible, right down to the very bottom where it's fucking dark and gloomy. But not now. They are all adults and I can't be responsible for ever.

And another thing is that the kids are really lovely. Cleaning up, making tea, responding to questions and conversations. They've grown up. I look at them both. Em is glowing with pregnancy. She has her hair tied back and has taken to wearing all of Caroline's maternity wardrobe despite it being — as far as I can tell — desperately uncool. She's not even wearing her hard-as-nails Doc Martens. Oscar is simply looking great. He's fresh, young, good looking (why he wants to cover that up with a fucking bear suit I still cannot explain but I'm not going there right now) and he knows stuff. It's a miracle, but he is following the environmental and political news just as much as Em and has a deep understanding of things that are going on.

But after both those things, lovely though they are, it probably helps my calmness that the hospital gave me some morphine tablets for the rib pain. Not strong ones, according to Em, but I take them a bit more often than I've been told to, and maybe slip an extra every so often. Whatever it is, or whatever combination of factors are making it so, I find this time with the family deeply relaxing.

It's good.

I don't want it to end.

18

It's a few months later, and I am in the habit of working late. It's something that happened probably due to not drinking in the evenings and having a purpose that seems to fit my skill set. I'm often last out of the office, but sometimes it's Vasi, and sometimes they come back to my flat to carry on working. They sit with headphones on usually listening to some awful rap or — frankly I don't know, I just imagine how awful it is.

"Hey, Jack." Vasi takes off his headphones. "Take a look at this. I've got it working." They grin. They're wearing the very same flowery dress they wore when I first met them. The full beard still bothers me a bit, I have to be honest, but ... you know ... each to their/theys/his/her/its own.

I pull up a chair. "You're a genius." I watch them twiddle a tablet playing a version of Asteroids. One that I've written in my evenings on the world's most unfashionable, but still working, computer, that will never ask to be updated.

Productive time in the evening is something utterly new to me. Well, maybe not completely new, but new since before I got married, if I can trust my old brain to remember that far back. And it's rewarding. I've re-enjoyed so much of the stuff I used to work and play with back when computers weren't connected to the internet and phones were push-button and wired.

I've been working on a few games, and Vasi came up with the idea of porting them to smart devices. "For the old fuckers," they says. They've got some grand plan of turning

201

it into a business by monetising nostalgia, and I'm all in. I've told them I don't want anything to do with it constantly worrying customers or sending emails or notification or reminders or updates — an ethical communication policy if you like — and Vasi thinks this innovative idea will be a selling point.

Innovation seems to come in all sorts of guises these days.

I've been seeing a lot more of the family and a lot less of Larry. For his part, Larry has become used to pouring a pint of soda water with a twist when I show up at the Flying Pig, and for my family's part they are often round at the flat. I've been over to help Caroline out with the odd bit of decorating or gardening or ... you know, just chats. It's been going well, but I'm not going to rush things so I have to avoid looking into those dreamy eyes of hers.

We are all mending — me in particular.

And then one night, sometime around 1 a.m. I get a phone call. My landline has been going gangbusters (as somebody once said, and I thought I'd try the phrase out to see if it works). But I've been in a deep sleep at the computer struggling with the graphics.

"Dad, it's Em. She needs us now. The baby's coming early."

"Fuck. Are you sure?"

"She's in pain, Dad. We need to get to hospital. I've been trying to call you."

"Call an ambulance. I'll be right over. Don't wait for me if it comes, I'll follow and meet you in hospital."

I don't know why he hasn't called for an ambulance instead of trying to wake me up. Sometimes bears are just fucking stupid. Thinking about honey, no doubt.

Shit. It would be this day, wouldn't it? I grab some

clothes and race to put them on while searching for car keys. Caroline said she'd only be away for the night, and would be back in town today. No risk of the baby coming; we still had a month to go. We'd even had the conversation, and now here I am at one o'clock on a freezing morning trying to find some clean pants and a set of car keys. Thank fuck I happened to have picked the car up yesterday, otherwise I'd be waiting for a taxi.

I get to the family house just as the ambulance arrives. The crew rush in to the house and ask me and Geronimo to keep clear. They don't bat an eye that Oscar is dressed up, and neither do I. It's all about Em. She's sweating profusely and looks clammy, cold. Her howls of pain grate the back of my neck.

"Is she going to be all right?"

"We'll get her to hospital, I'm sure she'll be fine."

They don't have time for a longer conversation, no matter how much me and Geronimo want it. We ask to go in the ambulance with her. They want us to go separately; we insist, they say no, we insist some more, but in the end we climb in the car and chase the ambulance through town.

Father and bear speeding round corners, cutting through red lights and mounting roundabouts to keep up with a blue light ambulance. It's not the sort of thing you expect to be doing on a Tuesday morning. And I probably won't have to do this again. Ever.

Geronimo's egging me on. "Faster Dad, you old bastard."

"I'm going as fast as I dare."

"Keep up, keep up."

He winds down the window and puts his bear head out. "Come on Dad," he shouts. "You're losing them." He bashes the dashboard with his paws.

In the scheme of moments or surreality, this is not up there with Dali's melting clocks or *Alice in Wonderland*. But I do think it rates somewhere between *Lucy in the Sky with Diamonds* and *Fear and Loathing in Las Vegas*. If we had time, I think we'd put on some rock music by AC/DC or Meatloaf to provide the soundtrack while we drove. But of course these moments can't be planned or they wouldn't be emergencies.

We race into the hospital just after the ambulance and I drop the bear at the door. He runs in behind the stretcher and disappears into the bright lights of A&E to accompany Em. I have to find a car park and put money in the meter, which even at this time of morning isn't easy. Fuck this government.

By the time I get into the hospital, Geronimo is standing near the reception desk being told to calm down.

"She's gone straight into surgery," he says. "Emergency C-section."

I start crying.

"Dad. It's okay, she'll be fine." The bear hugs me.

If you have ever been in this situation, waiting for news of a loved one in hospital, you'll know how it burns. It burns into your heart and when it's over, whatever the outcome, it burns into your memory. They are defining moments in life, like the first time you kiss, or the first time you get bullied — and subsequent times, actually — or your first shag, when you get married, or you go to a funeral. Our lives are punctuated by these moments and the tension is like a pen drawing on the map of your existence in permanent ink.

We wait. And every passing minute is full of heartache, fear and worry. It's more than fear, actually. It's petrification. Almost unable to move, to speak, to think.

People carry on around us as if it's all normal. Nurses go about their business, phone calls are made; some bloke gets a can of coke from the vending machine, but all these things sink into oblivion somewhere around the back of my mind where all the drains and sewage pipes take things away. They cannot compete. They are like ants compared to elephants.

We talk. About nothing. I don't remember the words; I just know words come out of my mouth and Geronimo responds to them. We must talk about coffee and something to eat because at some point a hot cuppa and a sandwich turn up. I don't know which one of us went to get them. Me or Geronimo. Probably me because they are cheese and pickle, not honey. Ha! It's not funny. Nothing is funny. And nothing is sad, nor jolly, nor mean, nor anything except burning pain.

And though this experience burns a deep memory into my brain, it can't last all that long because when the nurse appears to talk to us it's still dark outside.

"She's resting," says the nurse. "Mother and baby are doing fine."

She asks which of us is the father and stupidly I say, "I'm her father."

The nurse looks puzzled.

"Oh, the baby. No. No. I'm the mother's father."

So the nurse turns her attention to the listening bear. "You'll be able to see them soon."

"No. I'm the uncle," says the bear.

"Well. You can both go in shortly. For just a moment."

In the space of fifteen minutes, I go from terrified to in love, with only a short wait between while we finish our sandwiches and wait for the official nod. This contrast of mundane and extraordinary is one that will stay with me forever, and yet it happens to countless people in hospitals up and down the country every day.

We race up the stairs to the maternity ward, and when we finally meet the little chap he's red-faced and swaddled in crisp white blankets and wearing a tiny white cap. He's in a transparent plastic cot so everybody can see him from any angle. He's a small fellow, being only 3lbs and some change, but he is going to grow up to see some enormous changes. Just like I have, just like Geronimo continues to do and, well, just like everybody.

As we coo and stare, two things happen simultaneously. One, the door opens and Caroline bursts in, wet and flushed from running through the rain and up the two flights of stairs.

And secondly, Em wakes up.

We all look at her dotingly.

She takes a second to find her voice. "You've met him, then?"

"What's his name?" I ask.

Everybody freezes. They've discussed this and left me out of the conversation. It's clear.

"Oh! Dad. I didn't tell you," says Em.

Geronimo is deliberately staring down at the baby, and if Caroline could whistle I'm certain she'd be giving him her best rendition of 'You Are My Sunshine.'

"What's he called? Come on."

Silence.

"Come on. What's the big secret?"

Knowing looks between them all.

"It's Rupert," says Em.

Rolling eyes.

Jazz fucking hands.

THE END

A Personal Note

Please review this book.

Books take a long time to write, and then re-write, and then re-write again, and there is a considerable cost involved in producing a final version. It is a long, sometimes wonderful, but often difficult process.

If you have enjoyed this book, or even if you haven't, please leave a review on Amazon and Goodreads, or where you blog or post. Reviews can be life and death for books and for authors, and a review will help this book get noticed and hopefully pass on your enjoyment to others.

Thank you 😊

William Knight

THE DONATED

By William Knight

When techno-phobic journalist Hendrix 'Aitch' Harrison links bodies stolen from a renowned forensic research enclosure to a powerful pharmaceutical company, he suspects fraudulent manipulation of clinical trials.

With Doctor Sarah Wallace, a determined forensic entomologist, he delves into a world of grisly drug tests, misguided scientists and desperate patients pursing miraculous promises.

But with murderous interests arrayed against him, Aitch must battle more than his fear of technology to expose the macabre price of donating your final days to science.

"Powerfully written and thought-provoking. Highly recommended."
The Wishing Shelf Book Awards

"The science was mind blowing and the build to the story's climax was intense. You will read it thinking, 'Could this really happen?'"
bookstackreviews.com

"A strange, intriguing, and gripping novel."
Norman Bilbrough

Printed in Great
Britain
by Amazon